"Subtlety is the key....

"Just a soft brush of the lips," Simon continued, and before she could pull away he'd kissed Jaymie's fingers. "That's just the beginner's level, of course. The next step is to flip your hand over and kiss the palm...." His voice was slightly muffled as he demonstrated.

Jaymie pulled away.

"You seem a little flustered, Jaymie."

"Of course I'm not. Just ticklish." There was a catch in her voice.

Leigh Michaels has been a writer since she was old enough to figure out how to hold a pencil, but publishing a romance novel was an ambition she kept secret from everyone except her husband—her biggest supporter. They mailed her first manuscript together on Friday the 13th, which she says has been her lucky day ever since. She finds writing to be like tiptoeing into a parallel universe that's always waiting just around the corner from real life. All the people from all her books live there and sometimes interact in unexpected ways, making going to work every day a new adventure.

Leigh loves to hear from readers. You can write to her at P.O. Box 935, Ottumwa, Iowa, U.S.A. 52501-0935.

Books by Leigh Michaels

HARLEQUIN ROMANCE
3290—DATING GAMES
3300—A SINGULAR HONEYMOON
3311—TRAVELING MAN
3324—FAMILY SECRETS
3337—THE ONLY SOLUTION

HOUSE OF DREAMS
Leigh Michaels

Harlequin Books

TORONTO • NEW YORK • LONDON
AMSTERDAM • PARIS • SYDNEY • HAMBURG
STOCKHOLM • ATHENS • TOKYO • MILAN
MADRID • WARSAW • BUDAPEST • AUCKLAND

ISBN 0-373-03343-5

HOUSE OF DREAMS

Copyright © 1994 by Leigh Michaels.

This edition published by arrangement with Harlequin Enterprises B.V.

® and TM are trademarks of the publisher. Trademarks indicated with
® are registered in the United States Patent and Trademark Office, the
Canadian Trade Marks Office and in other countries.

Printed in U.S.A.

CHAPTER ONE

THE March wind roared across the hillside cemetery, slicing through Jaymie Logan's charcoal-colored wool coat and whipping a few tendrils of ash-blond hair which had escaped from the gray felt hat perched at the back of her head. She folded her arms across her chest and tried to focus on the pastor's words, but the canvas awning above her head snapped in the wind till she could hardly hear his deep, calm voice.

In any case, she didn't particularly want to listen. She was having enough difficulty in facing the fact that Gretta—infinitely warm and loving and funny Gretta—was gone, and the pastor's words were more likely to bring tears than comfort just now. For Jaymie, who much preferred to do her grieving in private, it was better not to think about Gretta until she was alone.

She bit her lip to try to hold back a sob and glanced around at the crowd. The mayor had come, and the superintendent of schools and the neighborhood handyman. Gretta Chadwick had known almost everyone in Summerset, and despite the bitter cold a great many friends and neighbors had gathered here today to say goodbye to her. A great many friends, but only one relative.

For the hundredth time that morning, Jaymie's gaze came to rest speculatively on Gretta's nephew. She hadn't chosen her position at the edge of the tent so that she could study Simon Nichols, but she couldn't have done better if she'd tried.

She had never seen him before today, except in Gretta's ever-present photographs. But even if Jaymie'd had no idea what to expect, it wouldn't have been difficult to pick him out. He was alone even in the center of this large crowd, for Gretta's friends maintained a respectful distance. There was nothing curious about that, since few of them had met him before. It was certain that hardly anyone here today could say they knew Simon Nichols.

He stood with his head bowed a little, hands clasped behind his back. He was wearing a black overcoat but no hat. The wind ruffled his dark, curly hair and created a tinge of red on his high cheekbones and his ears, but he seemed unaware of the cold.

Jaymie shivered a little and wondered if he was really as self-possessed as he seemed. She'd have to ask Gretta... Then the realization struck that she could never, never ask Gretta anything again, and her tears could no longer be denied.

The service ended. The pastor's final words rang out over the crowd, and for an instant total silence prevailed. Then he turned to Simon to offer a hand, and the crowd began to murmur and move toward the road where a long row of cars waited.

A hand closed on Jaymie's arm. 'I couldn't get near you in the church,' Holly Dermott whispered. 'Have you talked to him?'

Jaymie shook her head and fumbled for a handkerchief. 'He just got into town an hour before the service started.'

'When are you going to ask him?'

'Holly, I can't walk up to a man in the cemetery and say, Gee, I'm sorry about your aunt dying, and by the way can I borrow her house for a couple of months and open it up for tours?' The words were flippant, but her voice trembled.

'Don't make it sound so awful. Jaymie, you have to grab the chance. Herbert Anderson told me Simon's leaving later today.'

'If you're so eager, Holly, why don't you talk to him? I'm not the president of the Service League, you are.' But the protest was unreasonable, and she knew it. Talking to Simon Nichols about Gretta's house was Jaymie's job. And if he really was leaving Summerset before the day was out—and Herbert Anderson should know, for he'd been Gretta's lawyer—then Holly was right. There wasn't any time to lose.

Not that Jaymie was exactly surprised to hear that Simon wasn't planning to stay long. He'd never seemed to have much time for Gretta when she was alive, so why bother to stick around after her funeral was over?

Jaymie squared her shoulders with determination and turned back to the tent. Simon Nichols was gone.

She spotted him twenty yards away, heading toward the cars, and she rushed down the hillside. 'Mr Nichols!' The heel of her boot caught in an uneven spot in the frozen ground, and she almost plunged into him.

He had put out a hand to steady her, but she managed to regain her balance without leaning on him. His eyebrows lifted slightly. 'Yes?'

Jaymie hadn't realized how tall he was; at least six feet two, for she had to look up eight inches or so to meet his eyes. They were emerald-green, she noted, and his eyelashes were even darker and more curly than his hair. And there was a distinctive cleft in his chin.

'You were saying, Miss——?'

There was also something unusual about his voice. It was unexpectedly soft and deep enough to drown in...

'Jaymie Logan,' she managed finally. She could feel her cheeks warming; she hoped he would think it was only the friction of the wind which was causing the red flush and not embarrassment at being caught wool-gathering. 'I'm very sorry about Gretta.'

'Thank you. It's kind of you to come to the service.'

'She was my friend.' Her voice caught in her throat. 'Friend' was such a simple word, but it meant so very much, and she had to blink hard to keep the tears from overflowing again. 'Mr Nichols, I hate to trouble you at a time like this...'

She thought he almost said, Then don't, but he merely tipped his head politely.

Jaymie rushed on. 'But since I don't know how long you're planning to be in town... If you could spare me just a few minutes, I need to talk to you about Gretta and some unfinished business.'

'Miss Logan, this isn't the most pleasant place for a chat, and in any case I really don't have time.'

She wanted to ask him why he'd even bothered to come, if that was the way he felt. But she bit her tongue; she needed a favor, and attacking the man was no way to get it. 'It's important, Mr Nichols.'

'Then you might take the matter up with Herbert Anderson. He'll be handling the estate.'

'I already have, but Herbert felt I should speak to you.'

'Well, you've spoken to me.' Simon Nichols sounded almost soothing, as if he were talking to a child. 'And I'm delegating Herbert to deal with it.' He started to turn away. 'When I see him in a few minutes, I'll tell him he's authorized to take care of the matter.'

Jaymie reached out to grab his sleeve. His arm was like steel under the soft wool of his overcoat. 'It's about Gretta's house,' Jaymie said desperately.

'If you're interested in buying it, you certainly should talk to Herbert, not me. Until the estate is settled, he's in charge. Now I really must insist, because the entire crowd is being held up until my car moves. Good morning, Miss Logan.' He nodded politely and strode off toward the limousine at the head of the line.

She stared after him, astonished and too annoyed even to make her way to her own car. No wonder Simon Nichols hadn't seemed to feel the cold, Jaymie thought furiously. He'd been frozen solid long before he got to the cemetery!

Maybe it was just as well that he hadn't spent much time with Gretta. She'd have been heart-broken to have her illusions swept away...

Jaymie was so preoccupied that she didn't hear a voice shouting her name, and until Herbert Anderson took her arm she didn't realize he was beside her. 'I'm glad I caught you,' he said.

'Now what do you suggest I do, Herbert? You told me to talk to the iceberg there. I have, and he said I should take it up with you. He wouldn't even let me tell him what I wanted.'

'He's in a bit of a hurry, Jaymie.' Herbert sounded almost apologetic. 'He wants to leave as soon as possible, so I need you to come to Gretta's house right now.'

'Now?' Jaymie was startled. 'Do you mean *you* asked him?'

'About the Service League project? No, of course not. I'm asking you to come for the reading of the will.'

'Gretta's will? Why do you need me for that?'

'I can't tell you that right now,' the little lawyer said primly. 'All I can say is it was Gretta's wish for you to be present.'

'I suppose that means she left me books or jewelry or something?' Jaymie sighed. 'All right, Herbert, I'll be there as soon as I can.'

It took a quarter of an hour for the traffic to unsnarl; the old cemetery's gates were narrow and the street outside was a busy one. But eventually Jaymie made her

way into Summerset and to the house where Gretta
Chadwick had spent her entire life.

Just a block from the downtown business district, the
white brick Italianate mansion sat well back from the
street on a big, sloping lawn. At this season of the year
the only color came from the dull green junipers which
nestled low against the house, but in a month or so the
place would come alive with jonquils and tulips. They
would bloom just in time for the tours, Jaymie had
thought last fall when she and Gretta had first discussed
opening the Chadwick house to the public. Gretta so
loved her flowers, and she'd be so proud...

Jaymie groaned a little. Every time she caught herself
thinking of Gretta as if she were still alive, the pain got
worse.

Gretta wouldn't be there to see the flowers this spring,
Jaymie reminded herself almost harshly. And she
wouldn't get to help guide the tours, either.

Though it looked as if there would be no tours. Simon
Nichols hadn't even listened to her, and Jaymie suspected that if the decision was left to Herbert Anderson
he would opt not to rock the boat where his new client
was concerned. And, now that Jaymie had encountered
the man herself, she could understand Herbert's point
of view.

So she was left with a choice; she could drop the
subject altogether, or she could take advantage of this
second opportunity to try to convince Simon Nichols of
the worthiness of her cause. By bringing it up again, she
was taking the chance that Simon would refuse her
altogether, and she knew Herbert would never overrule
that decision. On the other hand, staying quiet and
hoping to talk Herbert into cooperating—perhaps by
suggesting to him that Simon Nichols might not even
have to know—seemed a bit underhanded.

Her grandmother's voice echoed in Jaymie's head. 'Whenever you have a choice, Jaymie,' she used to say, 'always opt for the truth. It's much less troublesome in the long run.'

But then Gran had never dealt with Simon Nichols...

And you haven't either, Jaymie reminded herself. Not really. It wasn't fair to judge the man based on two minutes' conversation on a windswept hillside as he was leaving his aunt's funeral. Once inside where it was warm, he might be perfectly reasonable.

The wrought-iron gates at the end of Gretta's driveway were open, but the drive was narrow, meant for the smaller vehicles of a much earlier day, and Jaymie had learned to negotiate it with care.

Though it had never been the grandest mansion in town, the Chadwick house had once been the cultural center of Summerset. The idea of a local symphony had been born there, over Gretta's grandparents' dinner-table. The little theater group had rehearsed in the space above the carriage house for years. And there was a story— but probably it was only a small-town legend, Gretta had said—that Enrico Caruso himself had slept in the guest room one night and given an impromptu concert in the front parlor.

Jaymie parked her car in front of the house. The tower room above the main entrance stood straight and proud and tall, though the elaborate brackets which decorated its overhanging roof were beginning to need paint. The delicate etched glass in some of the arched windows was original, and the double front doors were intricately carved. The interior woodwork had never been painted as it had in so many houses of the same vintage. And, though Jaymie happened to know that one section of the roof, flatter than the rest, suffered a persistent and so far untraceable leak which had annoyed Gretta for the last year, the house was in relatively good shape.

But through the years styles had changed. Summerset's retail district expanded toward the house, and newer neighborhoods climbed up the hills instead of nestling near the Summer River. Now the Chadwick house was isolated, almost surrounded by commercial development and protected only by its square block of grounds.

She rang the bell and listened with appreciation to the slow, sonorous chime which came clearly to her ears despite the thickness of the walls. They didn't make doorbells like that one any more.

One of the doors opened and a little woman peered out at Jaymie. Her gray hair was mussed, her eyes were red and a bit swollen, and she looked as if she hadn't slept in days. Jaymie wanted to put her arms around her and burst into tears herself, but Bess was so obviously trying to keep her head high that Jaymie had to respect her wishes. 'Hello, Bess,' she said. 'Mr Anderson asked me to come.'

Bess nodded. 'He said you'd be here for the will-reading. He hasn't arrived yet, but Mr Simon's in the library. I lit the fire in there as soon as I got back from the cemetery, so it'll be nice and warm in a few minutes. And I'll bring coffee as soon as it's finished perking.'

'That would be lovely.' Jaymie stepped into the main hallway and took her hat off. She hung it on the enormous mirrored coat rack and fussed with her hair, trying to push the loose tendrils into place in the twist at the back of her neck. Finally she gave it up, hung her coat on a hook, and smoothed her long rose-colored skirt. She might as well stop dawdling and take advantage of the opportunity to talk to Simon Nichols, because she was darned sure she wouldn't get another chance. And her time might be brief; she had no idea how many people might turn up today because they were included in Gretta's will.

The heels of her trim leather boots clicked against the checkerboard marble floor as she crossed the hall to the library. The door was half open, and she paused to take a deep breath before making her entrance. As if, she thought wryly, she were stepping onto a stage for the performance of her life.

The door swung silently, and she saw Simon Nichols standing by the fireplace, one elbow braced on the mantel, staring down at the small blaze crackling on the hearth. She wondered what he was feeling. Regret that he hadn't gotten to Summerset in time to see Gretta one last time? Or aggravation at this interruption to whatever was so important that he had to go rushing back to it today?

'Good morning, again,' she said crisply.

He jumped a little and turned his head, and energy seemed to crackle across the room. 'What are you doing here?'

'I was invited. Since it appears we have a few minutes to fill before Herbert arrives, perhaps you won't mind if I take up Gretta's unfinished business.'

'Who invited you?'

'Herbert did,' Jaymie said patiently. 'I don't know why. I suppose it means that Gretta left me her favorite bracelet. Shall we sit down?'

'You may if you like. I've already tried.'

Jaymie bit back a smile. She chose a chair with caution and perched on the edge of the leather seat. 'That's a good place to begin, actually. These are wonderful chairs——'

'Speak for yourself.'

'But the last time the springs were worked on, I'd guess, was sometime before the First World War. That one——' she pointed at a worn winged-back chair '—happened to fit Gretta's body perfectly, and so she didn't notice how uncomfortable it was for anyone else who sat there.'

Simon turned his back to the fire. There was a photograph of him at each end of the mantel, exactly level with his face; Jaymie thought it was almost like seeing him in triplicate.

'Would you mind getting to the point?' he asked.

'It took great effort for me to convince her that it was past time for the chairs—and the house—to have some professional attention.'

His eyes narrowed till she could hardly see they were emerald-green at all. 'I suppose that means you're an interior decorator?'

Jaymie thought irritably that he made it sound like something shady. Not actually criminal, perhaps, but definitely off-color. 'Yes,' she said crisply. 'I was doing some work for Gretta——'

'And that's the unfinished business you want to talk about?'

Jaymie finally realized what was so unusual about his voice. It was a very slight slurring of the vowels, as if he'd picked up a hint of a drawl somewhere.

'I suppose she agreed to an overhaul of the place, and then died. Well, I'm sorry, but that's the way business turns out sometimes.' His voice was matter-of-fact. 'Send Herbert a bill for whatever work can't be canceled, and that's the end of it.'

'That's *not* the end of it,' Jaymie countered. 'It's a lot more complicated than that. Gretta couldn't afford the kind of work this place needs, so we worked out a deal.'

He raised one eyebrow. Jaymie could feel his suspicion washing over her in waves.

'It's a fairly common arrangement.' She hurried on. 'The Summerset Service League does a big fund-raising project annually, and this year we settled on the idea of a showcase house.'

'I'm sure you'll explain that to me.'

'Of course.' At least he was listening, she thought. 'Several interior designers team up to redecorate a house, which is then opened to the public for tours for a few weeks. The ticket price goes to charity—in this case, the ones the Service League supports. The designers get a tax deduction for their contributions and all sorts of good advertising of their work. The public has a good time, and the homeowner gets a free redecoration.'

'And Gretta agreed?'

'Yes.'

'Did you have a contract?'

'Of course not,' Jaymie said wearily. 'I was dealing with a friend.'

'So now you're short of a house.'

'That's just about it, yes. But if you'll——'

'Look, I'm sure it's a good cause, and I'm sorry about the nuisance, but I don't see what I can do about it.'

Jaymie bit her lip. There was no reason, she reminded herself, why Simon Nichols should have the same kind of soft spot in his heart for a good cause that Gretta had. But perhaps an appeal to fairness would move him.

'We've already got all the materials,' she said. 'There's a bedroom full of paint and wallpaper upstairs. In fact, we'd have started work by now if Gretta hadn't become ill.'

'That's fortunate, don't you think? You can send everything back.'

'Not the special order items. In any case, we've already spent money we can't recover for things like advertising and publicity brochures.' She pulled a leaflet out of her handbag and held it out to Simon, but he didn't reach for it. Jaymie tossed the brochure onto the desk. 'We're calling it the House of Dreams,' she said. 'But at this rate it's turning into a nightmare. If we don't follow through on the project, the club will be in a serious financial hole, and our charities won't be funded at all.'

'Get another house.'

'There isn't time. The tours are set to begin on the first day of April, and that's only three weeks away. In any case, the materials we bought to use here wouldn't be adaptable for just any house.'

'I'm sorry,' he said, 'but——'

Bess came in with the silver coffee-tray. Her hands were trembling a little under the weight of it. Jaymie leaped out of her chair and swept a stack of books off the corner of Gretta's desk; Simon took the tray.

'Thank you,' Bess said. 'I don't know why, but that seems to get heavier every time I lift it.' She slipped out of the room.

There were three eggshell-thin cups and saucers on the tray. Apparently, Jaymie thought, they were not waiting for a crowd after all. And where was Herbert, if he wasn't gathering up the rest of the heirs? Was he deliberately giving her this opportunity to make her case to Simon? Thoughtful of him, if so. Not that it was doing any good.

'Cream and sugar?' she asked.

Simon shook his head. 'Nothing, thanks.'

'Do you mean no added ingredients,' Jaymie asked a bit tartly, 'or no coffee?'

He smiled. Jaymie half expected his face to crack, but it didn't. In fact, she had to admit, he looked rather pleasant when he wasn't glaring at her. 'Black,' he said.

Jaymie handed him a cup and saucer.

'Bess has been saying that ever since I can remember,' he mused. 'About the tray getting heavier.'

'She's been with Gretta a long time, hasn't she? What's going to happen to Bess?'

Simon shrugged. 'I'd suggest you not waste time worrying about it. I'm sure Gretta made arrangements.'

And what if she hadn't had time? Jaymie wanted to ask, but she reminded herself it was none of her business. If it was necessary, she'd work something out...somehow. Right now, she had other things to pursue. 'As I was saying, finding another house——'

Simon sighed. 'You never give up, do you?'

'Not when it's important. Changing to another house simply isn't possible at this late date. Not every family can just move out of its home on short notice for a couple of months. And not everyone can afford to pay a mortgage and rent on another place, too——'

'Oh? This organization of yours doesn't even pay rent?'

Jaymie would have liked to bite her tongue off. 'Well, no. But all the profits go to charity—and a complete redecorating isn't a minor benefit for the homeowner, you know.'

'It also isn't at the top of my priority list.' He refilled his coffee-cup and moved back to the fire.

'Gretta would have wanted this to go on, you know.'

He didn't answer, but the tilt of his eyebrows made it obvious that he had his doubts.

Jaymie tried another direction. 'What do you plan to do with the house, Mr Nichols?'

'Isn't the question a little premature? I haven't inherited it.'

Jaymie frowned a little. It hadn't occurred to her that Gretta might do anything else with the place; she'd never mentioned any other family—just Simon. 'Don't you know what your aunt intended to do with her property?'

'She's always indicated anything she had would come to me, but——'

'Then it's not a premature question. It's just not official yet. What are you going to do with the house?'

'Assuming, of course, that it doesn't have to be sold to settle Gretta's last bills...'

'Oh. I hadn't thought of that.'

'I thought perhaps you hadn't. At any rate it doesn't matter much. Since I've never considered living in Summerset, I suppose I'd sell it anyway.'

'Well, why didn't you just say so in the first place? Would you agree that at the moment the house looks pretty run-down?'

He glanced around as if he'd never seen the place before. 'The furnishings are worn, yes, but what that has to do with the house itself——'

'All right, as far as the library's concerned, you're correct.' She waved a hand at the mahogany shelves. 'The panelling needs a good cleaning, of course, and some new curtains wouldn't hurt, but that's about all. However, walk across the hall to the parlor and you'll see what I mean. The wallpaper's fading and peeling——'

'It has a right. It's probably been up for thirty years.'

'That's my whole point. With Gretta here, nobody really noticed—she had a way of filling the whole place with light.' Jaymie tried to swallow the lump in her throat. 'But putting it up for sale is a whole new playground. If people think a house has been neglected, or if all they can see is loads of work to be done, that's reflected in the price they're willing to pay.'

'And out of the goodness of your heart,' Simon said gently, 'you're willing to take care of that little problem for me. How sweet!'

'It's a good deal for both of us. Let the Service League spiff the house and the furnishings up for you, and in two months you'll get a whole lot more money out of the place—with no investment.'

'What if I don't want to wait around in limbo for two months?'

'You'll have to wait a while—it takes time to settle an estate, no matter how much of a hurry you're in. Besides, how much demand do you think there is for a house like this? There are lots of old houses around here, and not so many buyers. Why not let us use it in the meantime?'

'You seem doubtful that someone could fall in love with the place at first sight.'

'Oh, it's possible,' Jaymie conceded, 'but before people start counting out cash they're generally pretty thorough where old houses are concerned. Besides, have you calculated the odds against someone loving it *and* having the money available to buy it instantly?'

'I must admit you make an interesting point.'

Jaymie tried to press her advantage. 'The house will sell faster after it's been redecorated. And just think of the number of people who will be coming through, people who otherwise wouldn't see the place at all.'

Simon moved back to the coffee-tray and topped off his cup once more. 'Where did Gretta intend to live while she was out of the house? At least I assume she wasn't going to stay here through all the fuss and commotion?'

Jaymie glanced warily at him through her lashes. 'She was going to stay with me, and Bess was going to visit her family. Why?'

He didn't answer for a moment. 'I'm not surprised, I suppose. An elderly woman, a bit innocent, lonely... Perhaps she could even be described as naïve...'

After a moment of astonishment, Jaymie began to laugh. '*Naïve*? Are you talking about *Gretta*? For heaven's sake——'

'It must have seemed a very easy thing to take advantage of her.'

Jaymie gasped.

'For a good cause, of course,' he added smoothly. 'And no doubt she was flattered by the attention of a young woman who seemed to want to be her friend. You're... quite attractive.' His gaze drifted over her as if inspecting every thread of her tight-fitting jacket and long skirt—and the curves which lay beneath.

Jaymie jumped up. 'I have never been so insulted in my life!'

'Really?' The drawl was more pronounced. 'And I thought I was paying you a compliment.'

She decided not to give him the satisfaction of responding to that. 'Gretta—lonely? Hardly. But if you honestly thought she was lonely, why didn't you do something about it when she was alive? I've been Gretta's friend—and regardless of what you think, we *were* friends—for two years, and I've never even seen your face!'

He turned his head slightly, as if contemplating the photographs on the end of the mantel.

'Except in all these crazy photographs,' Jaymie added. 'And if you think sending her a picture once in a while substituted for coming to visit her——'

His voice crackled. 'Who asked you to pass judgment on my relationship with my aunt?'

Well, Jaymie thought, there went the last hope down the drain. Not that there'd been much chance of him cooperating in the first place, but she'd really messed it up now. She'd have to go back to Holly and tell her that the House of Dreams was dead. They'd have to figure out the finances, probably assess a special charge to each member to make up the budget shortfall, and start over to try to raise funds for the charities which depended on them.

And the good which Gretta had so badly wanted to do would never be. That was what hurt the most. In the last few years, Gretta hadn't been able to give much financial help, but she had always been generous with her time and effort, and she had wanted to make this last grand contribution to Summerset.

The library door opened and Herbert Anderson bustled in, briefcase in hand. 'That fire's certainly welcome,' he said cheerfully. 'And coffee too, I see. I'm sorry to be delayed, Simon; I know you're anxious to be on your way. But I had to stop and get the will from my safe, and you know how that goes. As soon as you set foot in the office everyone wants something.' He rubbed his hands over the fire and reached for the cup and saucer Jaymie handed him. 'Well, at any rate, you've had a chance to get acquainted. Have you had a nice chat?'

There was silence, and he looked from one to the other of them, his eyes bright with curiosity. 'Ah, yes, well. I suppose we'd best get down to business.' He pressed the bell next to the fireplace, then went around behind the desk and opened his briefcase. 'As soon as Bess joins us, we'll start.'

He must mean that Bess is named in Gretta's will, Jaymie thought. How I hope she left Bess the whole works! That would fix Mr Know-it-all Nichols . . .

Bess slipped in and stood quietly in the corner of the room. Jaymie motioned her to a chair, but Bess shook her head.

'Wise woman,' Simon said. He didn't move away from the mantel.

Herbert removed a long blue folder from his briefcase and opened it with a snap. It wasn't a thick document, no more than four or five pages, and he spread it out very deliberately on the desk blotter and began to read. '"I, Gretta Irene Chadwick of Summerset, Illinois, revoke my former wills and codicils——"'

Jaymie sat up a little straighter. Did that mean Gretta had made a new will recently? Or was it just a conventional phrase to take care of loose ends?

Herbert was saying something about Gretta's debts and funeral expenses; that, Jaymie knew, was a standard clause. When was he going to get to the interesting stuff? If Gretta had left everything she owned to Bess, what fun it would be to see the expression on Simon Nichols's face!

"'I direct that the following specific bequests be made from my estate,'" Herbert droned on. "'My bedroom furniture, including my four-poster and the matching wardrobe, nightstands and dressers shall be distributed to Jaymie Ann Logan.'"

A warm feeling settled softly around Jaymie's heart. Gretta's bedroom furniture was superb, and she'd been very proud of it. The idea that she'd wanted it to come into Jaymie's care helped just a little to soothe the pain of her loss. To give her the most intimate and personal of furniture... But that was like Gretta.

Of course, what Gretta had thought Jaymie would *do* with it was another story altogether. The wardrobe was eight feet tall and the four-poster bed almost ten, and they would never fit in Jaymie's apartment. Still, it was a magnificent gift, and surely someday she'd have a place where she could use it.

She didn't look at Simon Nichols, but she could feel him watching her, and she wondered what he was thinking. Irritation that such intensely personal items had gone to an outsider? Or glee that she hadn't been given more?

"'Also, the walnut coat tree in the front hall, the Boston rocker and the rose velvet parlor suite shall be distributed to Jaymie Ann Logan.'" Herbert gave her a smile of congratulations and turned the page.

Jaymie pressed her fingertips to the center of her forehead, where a tiny pain had started to throb.

Bless Gretta's heart, Jaymie thought, but her generosity was overwhelming. Didn't she realize that Jaymie had just three rooms and a bath? The furniture would have to go into storage, and the fees would crunch her budget before the year was out.

She could see, from the corner of eye, that the corner of Simon's mouth had quirked as if he was trying not to smile.

Herbert went on, '"The furniture in the back bedroom, commonly called Bess's room, shall be distributed to Bess Pomeroy in gratitude for her long service to me."'

Jaymie forgot her own concerns. Was that all? Twenty years' devotion and all Bess got was a sofa and a bed? That didn't sound like Gretta. 'Herbert, that can't be right.'

Simon frowned.

Herbert looked up. 'What is it, Jaymie?'

'Is that *all*? I mean, surely Gretta left Bess some money. It wouldn't be like her not to.'

Simon shifted his position by the fireplace. He looked restless, almost impatient.

That's just too bad, Jaymie thought. Bess was important, and they were going to discuss it now, no matter how eager Simon was to get out of Summerset.

'Miss Jaymie,' Bess said, 'it's all right. Really.'

'It is *not* all right——' Too late, Jaymie realized how embarrassed Bess must be by this discussion, and she sank back into her chair. 'I'm sorry, Bess. I didn't think. We'll talk about it later.'

Bess smiled and her eyes filled with tears. 'It's sweet of you, Miss Jaymie, but Miss Gretta took care of all that. She arranged a pension for me.'

Simon looked at Jaymie as if to say, See? I told you not to worry about it.

Herbert cleared his throat and looked down at the will once more. 'I direct that my residual estate shall be distributed to my nephew, Simon Chadwick Nichols, of Atlanta, Georgia.'

Atlanta? No wonder he has a drawl, Jaymie thought.

She let her mind drift while Herbert droned on about the way the estate would have been split had Simon not survived his aunt. There hadn't been any big surprises after all. Simon got everything else Gretta had owned— or, as he had pointed out, whatever was left of it after the bills and estate taxes had been paid. The furniture, the personal property, the cash, the house...

And so, as soon as this interminable exercise was finished, Jaymie would call Holly Dermott and they'd put their heads together and decide what to do about the showcase project.

If only there were another house! Maybe the people who owned the bed and breakfast would like a redecoration. That was an old house, much the same period as Gretta's, and some of the wallpaper and paint would be adaptable. But she was certain they couldn't afford to close down their business for a couple of months...

"'I nominate Jaymie Ann Logan——'" Herbert said.

Jaymie sat up straight. 'What?'

'—to be my executor, and direct that she serve without bond——'

Executor, she thought in stunned disbelief. Gretta had named Jaymie to be the person who finished up the details of her life, straightening out the bills, paying the debts, tracking down the property, selling the excess, paying the taxes, filing the forms, and ultimately distributing everything to the heirs. It was a thankless but necessary job, and usually it was given to the person who was most involved in the estate—the closest relative of the deceased. Simon Nichols, in other words.

So why in heaven's name had Gretta chosen Jaymie instead?

CHAPTER TWO

JAYMIE'S mind was swimming with confusion. If there had been several heirs, of course it would make sense to name an outsider as executor, rather than single out one of them. That would prevent unfairness—or, perhaps even more important, the perception that the executor was arranging things for his own benefit rather than the good of all. But Simon was the only heir. What harm could it do to let him handle the paperwork and the details of his own inheritance?

'What in heaven's name was Gretta thinking of?' Jaymie snapped. 'It's insane to drag me into this mess!'

'My very thought,' Simon muttered. 'At last we've found *something* we agree on.'

Jaymie swung around to face him and was startled by his expression. He looked as if he'd bitten into something poisonous, and just seeing that look caused a little curl of resentment deep inside her stomach. Why should Simon Nichols be so adamant, anyway? She'd asked him for a favor, that was all—surely there was nothing wrong with that. And she'd been given a few pieces of furniture, which were clearly Gretta's, to dispose of. It wasn't as if she'd walked off with his entire inheritance!

Herbert paused and cleared his throat and seemed to debate whether he should get involved in the squabble. Eventually, he continued reading instead. 'And I direct that in addition to other powers and authority granted by law the said Jaymie Ann Logan shall have the right and power to lease, sell, mortgage or otherwise encumber any real or personal property that may be included in my estate, without order of court and without notice to anyone.'

Simon pushed himself away from the mantel and bent over the desk. 'Let me see that! Herbert, are you incompetent or what? Don't you realize this says she can dispose of things any way she wishes?'

'You're the one who said you wanted to sell the house,' Jaymie reminded him. 'And as for the other stuff, you hardly seem the sentimental sort.'

'There are controls, Simon,' Herbert put in. 'It's a standard arrangement. And I'm sure Jaymie will consult you before taking any major action. If you'll just——'

Simon went straight on. 'And what does Gretta mean, "without bond"? There isn't an ounce of protection for the estate if she embezzles every cent Gretta had!'

'How *dare* you——?' Jaymie bit back the rest of the comment. 'Besides, what are you talking about, "every cent Gretta had"? It's not like this is a magnificent estate.'

'And how do you know so much about Gretta's financial affairs? Have you already been poking around in her papers?'

Jaymie stared at him. Her lower lip was trembling, despite her best efforts to control it. Not that she thought it would matter to Simon Nichols; he probably thought she was doing it on purpose! 'I told you I was her friend. She shared things with me.' She saw the doubt in his eyes and added defensively, 'How do you think I knew she couldn't afford to redecorate this place? Gretta told me, of course. Besides, you said yourself the house might have to be sold to pay the bills, so don't accuse me of being nosy!' She turned to Herbert. 'Do I have to be involved in this? Can I just say no?'

'Of course you have a choice,' Herbert said slowly. 'You can refuse the nomination, and the court will appoint another executor. But before you make up your mind, perhaps I can cast some light on Gretta's reasons for naming you.'

'I doubt it,' Simon said.

'I advised her to choose a local person,' Herbert began. 'Knowing that you were so far away, Simon, and so involved in your own responsibilities, I thought it doubtful you'd want to be saddled with the petty details.'

'Thanks for having my well-being at heart. That still doesn't explain why Gretta chose *her*.'

'My name,' Jaymie said sharply, 'is not difficult to pronounce.'

Simon glared at her. 'Why Miss Logan? Why not you, Herbert?'

The attorney shrugged. 'I'm already involved, you see, and, though I could be the executor as well, it's really a much better idea to have a different person. Besides, the cost to the estate of having an attorney care for all the details would be much larger than——'

'Oh, yes. Cost,' Simon said. 'I thought we'd get to that sooner or later. What does the executor stand to get out of this?'

Jaymie wasn't listening. She was thinking, Gretta, why did you drag me into this? And how soon can I get out of it? Though on the other hand...

'Jaymie will be reimbursed for her expenses, of course. And she'll be compensated for her time with a small percentage of the estate's proceeds.'

'Not bad work if you can get it,' Simon said admiringly.

'Herbert,' Jaymie said, 'read that once more, would you? The part about the real estate, I mean.'

Simon groaned. 'Please, do I have to hear it again?'

'As a matter of fact, I'm not finished with the will.' Herbert reread the section on the executor's powers and went straight on. The remainder was mostly legal mumbo-jumbo, Jaymie thought, and she waited patiently till he'd finished the last whereas and here-tofore. The only thing she found terribly interesting was the date; Gretta had written this will barely a month before she died.

'If the executor has the power to sign leases,' Jaymie said thoughtfully, 'then I could decide to lease the house to the Service League for a couple of months, couldn't I?'

Simon threw himself into Gretta's favorite chair. The springs protested, and he winced. 'Oh, why not do it up big? Just sell them the house and furnishings for a dollar, and then you can redecorate to your heart's content every year.' There was no surprise or shock in his voice, just sarcasm.

Obviously, Jaymie thought, he'd beaten her to the idea of the lease. He might even have hoped she wouldn't think of it herself. 'And Simon can't stop me?'

Herbert considered. 'Of course he could bring a lawsuit to prevent you from taking such an action.'

Simon sat up a little straighter.

'But as long as you've made a reasonable business de-cision—no selling valuable property for a dollar, mind!—the court would have no cause to refuse you permission. It might take months to be sure you've found all of Gretta's assets and debts, and the estate will have to stay open till then anyway. Renting the house for a short period would make perfect sense, especially since re-decoration would improve the chances of selling it in the long run.'

Jaymie shot a look at Simon. 'What did I tell you?' she said under her breath.

'You've got Herbert buffaloed, too? Why are you so sure redecorating will be an improvement? Maybe people want an *untouched* old house.'

Jaymie ignored that. 'And if Simon sues me, the lawsuit would take a lot longer than a couple of months to resolve, wouldn't it?'

'Probably so, yes,' Herbert admitted.

'Then I accept Gretta's wish for me to be her executor. And the House of Dreams goes on as a memorial to her, to her wish to do one last wonderful thing for the community she loved.' Jaymie stood up and turned to face Simon, her shoulders squared. 'I'll show you, Simon Nichols. At the end of the two months I'll put the house up for sale—and you won't recognize it.'

'That's partly what I'm afraid of,' he muttered.

'And when you see the price it brings, maybe you'll even thank me, Simon. I can call you Simon—can't I? Now that we're going to be working together?'

'Oh, certainly,' he said smoothly. 'I'll take it as an honor.'

'And just as soon as it can legally be done,' she went on softly, 'the estate will be completed, and you'll get every single red cent that's coming to you. I won't even charge a fee—using the house is the only payment I want.'

Simon's eyebrows went up just a fraction. 'Why do I suspect that won't turn out to be quite accurate?'

'I'll leave you to discuss the details, then,' Herbert said briskly, and started to push papers back into his briefcase. 'Stop by my office tomorrow, Jaymie. There are some papers to sign before you can begin.'

'I'll go with you and take care of it right now.' Jaymie looked back as she reached the door. He hadn't moved; he was still sitting in Gretta's chair, his hands clasped on his knee. He was looking at Jaymie, and there was a light in his emerald eyes that jolted her. If he'd looked resentful, she wouldn't have been surprised, but there wasn't a trace of that. Instead there was speculation in that level green gaze. And something just short of a challenge.

She shivered despite herself, and wondered if she'd taken on more than she could handle.

Early in Summerset's history, the warehouse district which lined the banks of the Summer River had been the center of commerce, bustling with traffic and bulging with goods shipped by barge. Then the traffic had shifted from river to railroad, and the big old warehouses had stood empty and ignored for decades. Now the district had come to life again with a different kind of commerce; the warehouses had been linked together in a chain by glass corridors and skywalks to form a giant shopping mall. The rough bricks had been cleaned and tuck-pointed, new windows looked out on courtyards, and atriums soared through the center of each building, inviting the weary shopper to rest a while.

Jaymie ignored the subtle invitation of the splashing fountain and park benches just outside the door of Summerset Interiors. It was unusual for her to pay no attention to the atmosphere, for she'd carefully chosen this prime corner location three years ago when she'd started her business. In fact, she'd deliberately passed up a larger space on a higher floor in order to afford this particular corner.

And so far, it seemed, her judgment was paying off. Most of her work involved custom orders, so she didn't need space for an enormous inventory. Anyway, she couldn't afford to keep a lot of merchandise on hand, even if she wanted to.

Which she didn't, because the kind of striking display which drew clients into a business to look wasn't at all the sort of thing they wanted to live with. So Jaymie limited herself to small and exquisite arrangements in the shop's single window. She had turned most of the floor space over to fabric samples and photographs, and arranged what should have been her office as a tiny sitting-room—a comfortable place for clients to sit and chat and sip coffee and browse through books.

Still, it was hard for the untrained eye to visualize from photographs and samples such things as how a particular fabric would look on a chair, how well the chair would show off next to the fireplace, and whether the hearthrug would be better in a different shade. That was one of the reasons Jaymie had been so enthusiastic about the idea of a showcase house. Besides, a real house was better than any amount of raw display space, because it was a thousand times easier for clients to appreciate the whole effect.

Her assistant was pulling discontinued fabric samples from a display rack, with the telephone balanced between her shoulder and her ear. When Jaymie came in, Connie looked relieved. She didn't even bother with a greeting, just cupped her hand over the mouthpiece and muttered, 'Holly Dermott. She's called three times this afternoon.'

'Thanks, Connie.' Jaymie went into her office and closed the door before she took the cordless telephone from the drawer of the tea table which served as her desk. 'Sorry I wasn't here, Holly. You wouldn't believe what happened.' She slid out of her coat and tucked it behind a screen in the corner of the room.

'He wasn't cooperative, hmm?'

Jaymie laughed. 'You could say that.'

'Well, I've called an emergency meeting of the Service League for tonight.'

'Good. We need to get the details ironed out before we can start work on the house.'

'You pulled it off?' Holly shrieked. 'But I saw him walk away from you in the cemetery. Everybody who was there saw it.'

'That was only the beginning of a long negotiation.'

A smile warmed Holly's voice. 'That sounds very interesting. So tell me, what did you have to give up?'

'Well, I can almost guarantee that by the time this is done I'll have an ulcer.' Jaymie had had no idea till she'd started signing papers in Herbert's office what she was getting herself into; she certainly hadn't been given the kind of no-strings-attached freedom that Simon seemed to expect she was getting.

'Oh? Is Simon staying around, then?'

'No, thank heaven. He's on his way back to Georgia.' Jaymie heard the discreet chime which said the front door had been opened. 'I've got a customer, Holly, I've got to go. Where's the meeting?'

'My house. Seven o'clock.'

'All right, I'll see you then.'

She slid the phone into the drawer and ran a hand across her hair. It was getting close to closing time, so she hoped the customer wasn't someone wanting to spend hours browsing for ideas.

Connie had just put her hand on the office doorknob when Jaymie opened the door. Jaymie looked over the woman's shoulder at a man—tall, with dark curly hair and emerald eyes.

'I thought you were anxious to get back to Atlanta.' To her dismay, her voice wavered.

Simon didn't seem to notice. 'Not as eager as I was earlier in the day.'

'If you're going to try to talk me out of being Gretta's executor, it's too late. I've already signed the papers.'

'I wouldn't bother to try anything so obviously doomed to failure.'

The curt note in his voice affected Jaymie like fingernails on a blackboard, and she raised her chin a half-inch in defiance. 'Not that you'd be much happier with a substitute, I expect. Herbert told me the court would probably name Gretta's bank, and trust departments are notorious—they're far more apt to call in an auctioneer than to ask what things the heirs are sentimentally attached to.' She picked up a book of tapestry samples and hung it in place on the rack.

'And you would ask?'

She was startled at the question. 'Of course I would.' Did he really think she'd dispose of Gretta's things without even consulting him? Perhaps he was a bit more sentimental than she'd thought.

Simon was silent for a long moment. 'Look, Jaymie, I was taken by surprise this afternoon, and I'm willing to concede that I said a whole lot more than I should have. I'm sorry for that.'

He didn't sound sorry, but for the moment even a half-hearted apology was a great deal more than she'd expected. Jaymie looked him over slowly. 'But you still think you're right, don't you?'

'Of course I do. You're completely inexperienced, you're an outsider——'

'And in your opinion I've already taken advantage of Gretta's good nature, so why wouldn't I help myself to the estate?'

'That too. Don't get the idea of using whatever's left of Gretta's money to pay for this remodelling, or you'll be hauled up in front of a court so fast you won't believe it.'

'I'm delighted you think I'd only steal to support the remodelling, not for myself,' Jamie said sweetly.

'Isn't it the same thing? And don't get the idea I'm giving up. I've just decided to let you have the bother of doing all the paperwork.'

'Thanks a bunch.' Jaymie's voice was dry.

He smiled just a little. 'You're quite welcome. Now, with that understanding, perhaps we can sit down and talk about Gretta and the estate.'

Jaymie's first reaction was to tell him to get out of her shop. On second thought, she concluded that she'd better grab the opportunity. Next week she'd have to find him before she could even ask a question.

Jaymie looked around. Connie had discreetly moved into the office, and she could see the month's invoices spread out on the tea table. She hated to ask the woman to interrupt her work once again, but the showroom was no place for a conversation. Closing time or not, someone was bound to come in soon.

Simon seemed to read her mind. 'I'd like another cup of coffee. Isn't there a restaurant somewhere in the mall?'

Jaymie nodded. 'I guess I can slip out a little early.'

Riley's wasn't the usual fast-food place; it was a full-service restaurant with a restful air, wide-spaced tables, and spotless linen, located well out of the traffic pattern at the extreme end of the chain of warehouses which formed the mall. In the late afternoon, it wasn't busy, and the hostess showed them to a choice table by the window, with a view of the Summer River.

Simon looked around the room and then glanced at the menu. 'This is a very restful atmosphere,' he said.

'Thank you.'

He looked a bit startled.

Jaymie was gratified. 'This room is a new expansion, just opened last year. I decorated it.'

His drawl was a little more pronounced than usual. 'Is that my cue to challenge your professional qualifications, and then you'll defend yourself and shred my character and we'll be right back where we started?'

'I didn't say anything of the——'

'You didn't have to. I told you, I was taken by surprise earlier. Now that I'm not surprised any more, I'm not going to argue with you.'

That voice of his, Jaymie thought absently, was the audible equivalent of bedroom eyes. Slow and warm and sexy—she supposed some women might actually like that sort of thing.

'It's very nice,' he added. 'Unusual, though. Most restaurants don't want you to be so comfortable that you sit and drink coffee for hours. They'd rather turn the table and get another customer in.'

Jaymie shrugged. 'Relaxed and peaceful is what the owner wanted, and I always work with the client's wishes.'

'Always?' he asked thoughtfully. 'That's interesting. Since at the moment I could be considered your client...'

'That's only a technicality till the estate's settled, so don't get ideas.'

Simon shrugged as if he was unconvinced.

Jaymie hurried on before he could make an issue of it. 'I think I'll order a sandwich, too. I didn't feel much like eating lunch.'

'Neither did I.'

Jaymie was startled by the flat, quiet tone of his voice. For the first time, she saw nothing in his eyes but understanding and a pain which corresponded to her own. Had she underestimated his feelings for Gretta? The question rocked her; she didn't want to look further into it. But she couldn't seem to tear her gaze away from his.

Then, abruptly, she felt as if shutters had been slammed over his feelings; his eyes narrowed a bit, and his tone was once more slow and soft. 'Are the Reubens good?' he asked.

'The best in town.'

Simon glanced around and the waitress hurried over. Jaymie asked for a vegetarian special and separate checks; Simon ordered the Reuben and told the waitress to put everything on one bill.

Jaymie settled back in her chair and stirred her coffee. 'Goodness, we are making progress, aren't we?'

'Because I'm buying your dinner?' There was an ironic gleam in his eyes. 'Maybe I should give the bill to you. After all, your expenses are being reimbursed by the estate.'

Jaymie shook her head, refusing to rise to the bait. 'I wouldn't consider this a necessary expense. I meant that you actually took my word about the Reubens.'

It was the first time she'd seen him really smile, and Jaymie was startled. This was no half-smothered quirk, but a wide and generous grin which set white teeth gleaming, laugh-lines crinkling, and emerald eyes sparkling. The combination left her feeling rather faint.

He was one very handsome man, she thought. Between the looks and the voice...it was just too bad the inside of him wasn't as attractive as the exterior.

She cleared her throat. 'Perhaps you can start by telling me which things you want from Gretta's house.'

'Now?'

'Not this moment, no. Don't you think it would be better for both of us if everything was in writing?'

'A little self-protection, Jaymie?'

'Do you blame me? In fact, it wouldn't be a bad idea for you to make two lists. Things you want, and things you definitely don't want.'

He looked at her in disbelief. 'You expect me to list everything in the whole house?'

'Of course not. If something isn't on either list, I'll ask. But that way I won't have to call you over every piece of furniture. Satisfied?'

'Yes, ma'am,' he said. The words were meek, but his tone was not.

Jaymie ignored the underlying cynicism. She was going to do her job the best way she could, and eventually he'd have to admit that she was sincere. 'There's no particular rush. Gretta and I had already agreed that whatever furniture and knickknacks the decorators didn't want to use in the showcase would simply be stored till the tours were over. I'll wait till I hear from you before I dispose of anything.'

'Or before you change it?'

'You mean recovering chairs and such? Why are you so dead set against the idea of the showcase house?' She looked at him thoughtfully over the rim of her cup. 'If it's the idea of people trailing through the family mansion that you don't like, Simon, you'd better get used to it. As soon as the house is listed for sale, they'll be going through in troops.'

Simon's eyes turned to steel. 'I thought you said it would be tough to sell.'

'And I haven't changed my mind,' Jaymie said patiently. 'I'm just pointing out that there's a lot of curiosity about that house, especially in the last few years since Gretta hasn't held so many club meetings and events there. People will ask for showings whether they're interested in buying the house or not.'

'Isn't there anything more fascinating to do in Summerset than that? What do you do with your spare time, Jaymie?'

She sighed. 'I don't expect to have any for the next few months.'

The waitress brought their sandwiches. Jaymie carefully gathered up her vegetarian special—though it tasted good, it was one of the messiest things on the menu—and took a bite.

Simon sampled his Reuben. 'You're right, that's very good.'

'Must you sound so surprised?' The smile she had half expected didn't materialize, and Jaymie was startled to find herself feeling disappointed. Idiot, she thought. As if she actually cared whether Simon smiled at her!

'Why did Gretta choose you?' he asked. 'Herbert's explanation doesn't hold water, you know. Naming someone in Summerset might be reasonable enough, but why should it be you?'

Jaymie shrugged. 'Maybe she suspected she wouldn't live long enough to finish the project, but she wanted the showcase house to go on and she knew I'd take care of it.'

'Then why didn't she just say so?'

'How should I know? Maybe she felt silly talking about premonitions. And that's all it could have been, because her last illness came up so suddenly.'

'So instead of telling me what she wanted she called up Herbert and went through all the effort of changing her will? That's not my idea of a real time-saver, Jaymie.'

So Simon had noticed the date on the will, too.

'And if that's how she felt,' he went on, 'then why didn't she specify in the will that the showcase was to continue, instead of just naming you as executor?'

'I don't know, Simon. But if she'd simply told you, you wouldn't have been required to go along with her wishes.'

His jaw tightened, and every hint of the drawl was gone from his voice. 'The same way you're not required to follow them.'

'That's not what I meant,' Jaymie said uneasily.

'If Gretta had asked me for anything within legal boundaries, I'd have done it, no matter what it involved—and she knew it.'

Jaymie drew back in her chair a little, realizing for the first time that perhaps it wasn't her he resented so much as Gretta. She could understand his anger, for even if Gretta's motive had been the best—trying to save him frustration and work—it must have stung to have so much control taken away from him and given to someone he didn't even know.

Still, she couldn't stop herself from saying, 'Maybe she tried. You're not the easiest man in the world to get hold of, you know. Herbert told me he called every number in Gretta's address book before he finally made connections with you.'

'And by then she was gone,' Simon said wearily. He rubbed his hand across the back of his neck as if it hurt. After a bit, he said, 'Were you with her?'

'Not at the end. I stopped by the hospital whenever I had a few minutes, but she was supposed to be getting better, you see. If I'd known—but the end was so fast, Simon. The nurses called me, but by the time I got there——' Her voice broke and she fumbled for a handkerchief, remembering the still room, the quiet little shape on the bed.

The hostess seated a couple nearby, and the woman called a greeting to Jaymie, eyed Simon with interest, and maneuvered an introduction. By the time the bustle had died down, Jaymie had control of herself again and was determined to change the subject. 'What business are you in, anyway?'

'Pizza.'

'Pizza?' She was momentarily stunned, and then she remembered his comments about the atmosphere at Riley's, and the professional terms he'd used. 'You mean like a restaurant?' she said weakly. 'I thought Gretta said something once about you being in finance.'

Simon shrugged. 'I run the cash register now and then. Maybe that's what she meant. I also clear tables and toss pizza crust and mop floors and do whatever else needs doing.'

A clump of sprouts had fallen out of Jaymie's sandwich. She frowned as she pushed the sprouts around on her plate with her fork. She'd have said, herself, that Simon wasn't the sort to be tossing pizza crust, much less mopping floors. There was a take-charge attitude about him that didn't mix well with that kind of work. But maybe he meant he was in charge of the place; a skilled manager would be right on the scene, taking care of details... And why should it matter to me? she wondered.

'Is it good pizza?' she asked finally.

He looked surprised. 'Of course. Next time you're in Atlanta, try it out.'

'I don't get down there often. The last time was almost ten years, and then we just drove through on the way home from Disney World—my parents and little brother and I.'

'Next time you should stay longer. It's a terrific city.'

He started to tell her about Atlanta, and by the time the waitress came to remove their empty plates Jaymie was startled to see how much time had passed. If anyone had told her earlier this afternoon that she would actually enjoy spending an hour with Simon Nichols, she'd have laughed till she was hysterical. As it was, she actually considered having dessert, even though she really didn't have time, just so that she could sit with him a little longer. And if that wasn't an idiotic thing to do...

'I really have to go,' she said. 'I have a meeting.'

Simon nodded and reached for the bill. 'I'll leave my list on Gretta's desk.'

'You mean now? Tonight? I thought you'd be catching a plane.'

'What plane did you have in mind?' he asked drily. 'I missed the afternoon commuter, and the next flight out of this incredible town isn't till nine in the morning.'

'Oh.' She felt like a fool for forgetting that. 'Do you need a ride to the airport?'

'Are you trying to make sure I get out of town? No, thanks, I'll call Herbert. I need to talk to him again anyway.'

'Then from now on we'll be dealing by telephone.'

His eyes sparkled. 'Don't try so hard to sound pathetic about how much you'll miss me,' he recommended.

Jaymie snapped, 'I'm only hoping the number Herbert gave me is the one that actually works!'

'I'll write it down for you, just in case. And don't get your hopes up. I'll be keeping an eye on you, Jaymie...one way or the other.'

CHAPTER THREE

JAYMIE'S parents' house was a neat little ranch on a corner lot in a middle-class neighborhood that was comfortable but unpretentious. She parked by the garage door, knowing that both her parents would be gone to work by now. But at the side of the driveway sat a beat-up old car, its exterior a patchwork of multicolored paint and body putty. That meant Jaymie was in luck, for her brother hadn't left for his classes at the college yet. In fact, Rob was no doubt still in bed.

Rather than knock and wait for him to rouse and let her in, Jaymie used her key to the back door. She was in the kitchen, writing a note to her mother about the bulletin board she wanted to borrow from the room that had been hers till a few years ago, when Rob appeared, his hair still wet from the shower.

He breezed past, patting Jaymie on the head as casually as if she were his Irish setter, and dropped a thick slice of bread into the toaster. 'How about giving me a lift to school, James?'

Jaymie finished her note and stuck it on the microwave door. 'What's wrong with your car?'

'I hit a rock out by Paradise Valley last night and knocked a hole in the exhaust system.'

'How could you tell?' Jaymie was honestly interested. 'On its best days that car sounds like an army tank.'

'It got even noisier,' Rob said simply. 'And I suspect it's leaking exhaust fumes. Since I don't have the funds to fix it till I get my paycheck next week . . .' He sat down at the breakfast-bar, long legs sprawling, and began spreading grape jelly liberally over his toast.

'How did you plan to get to school if I hadn't turned up?'

'I don't know. Hitchhike, maybe, or roll the windows down and drive very carefully.'

Jaymie shuddered at the thought of carbon monoxide. 'All right, Rob. One ride to school, but that's it. I'm not a taxi service.'

'Gee, thanks, James.' Rob's voice dripped irony. 'Your generosity overwhelms me.'

'I'll also loan you the money to fix the car.'

His eyebrows soared. 'On second thought, I take it back. You know, sometimes it's not so bad having an older sister hanging around the house.'

'I should get that in writing while I can,' Jaymie muttered. 'And in certain circumstances I won't even insist that you pay it back.'

Rob stopped munching and looked at her warily. 'Like what circumstances?'

'I need a good set of muscles at the Chadwick house every evening this week, to move furniture and stuff like that.'

He flexed his biceps like a wishful Mr America, but he said, 'I don't know, James. The Chadwick house? Tommy says it's haunted.'

'What? Why would he say something like that?'

'He saw lights moving in the tower room at midnight last night. There were never lights up there before Gretta died. And it was the stroke of midnight, too—don't you think that's suggestive?'

'Of course not. It's only a storeroom, after all, and there was seldom any reason for Gretta to go up there at all, much less after dark—so obviously no one ever saw lights. And Bess had enough trouble with the regular stairs, so she avoided those narrow little twisting steps up to the tower unless she absolutely had to go there.'

Rob sounded unconvinced. 'Then why did Tommy see lights last night? Who was up there, if it wasn't a ghost?'

'Simon, I suppose. Though what he was looking for in the tower is beyond me.' Jaymie went to get the bulletin board from her room. Simon, she suspected, had been trying to do a complete inventory of Gretta's possessions, down to the last box in storage. As if he thought that Jaymie would abscond with any items which he didn't put on one list or the other!

She found the bulletin board not in the room which had been hers, but in Rob's. It was plastered with photos. She didn't look closely, but the contents seemed an even split between snapshots of his male buddies and young women in swimsuits. He'd even glued photos to the wood frame, so she gave up the idea of using the board as a message center at the Chadwick house. They'd have to make do with something else instead.

She followed Rob the few blocks to the muffler place to drop off his car, then gave him a ride to the college campus, and he promised faithfully to turn up at the Chadwick house after his last class for the day. 'Always assuming I can catch a ride with someone,' he added mournfully. 'If I have to walk all the way downtown it'll take lots of time.'

Jaymie refused to feel sympathetic; Rob's friends numbered in the hundreds, and surely on any given day at least one of them had a car which would run. 'The sooner you turn up to work, the earlier you'll be done,' she pointed out. 'In other words, you can be out of there before Tommy's hypothetical ghost has a chance to get restless.'

'Maybe I'll bring Tommy. With double the hands, the work will go faster.'

'And the payback time for your loan will double too, if I'm paying both of you.'

'Slave-driver,' Rob muttered. But he gave her a good-natured grin and an affectionate punch in the arm as he slid out of the car.

Rob was a nice kid, Jaymie thought as she back-tracked toward the center of town. As brothers went, he wasn't bad at all—now that she'd moved out and didn't have to cope with him on a daily basis.

The mall wouldn't open for almost another hour, so she had time to stop at the Chadwick house and check out some details. At the Service League meeting last night, a couple of the decorators had said they planned to start work today, so Jaymie needed to look over those rooms to be certain that Gretta's personal items had been removed. And then there was her own work to be started. She'd signed on for several rooms, mostly the troublesome ones—like the kitchen—which would soak up hours and funds but not make the spectacular, photogenic splash that a well-decorated foyer or living-room would.

But then, she reminded herself, she'd had the best motives in the world when she'd chosen to pick up the loose ends that the other decorators didn't want to tackle. She was doing the work for Gretta's sake. And now that Gretta was gone and the House of Dreams would serve as her memorial...

She still believed that her first instinct had been right, and that Gretta had named her as executor so that the showcase could go on. Not only for the sake of the Service League's charities, Jaymie thought, but because it would be better for the house.

Gretta must have realized how unlikely it was that Simon would bother himself over an old house in Summerset. Gretta had anticipated that he'd want to get rid of it as quickly as possible, and so she had arranged for Jaymie to take care of the matter instead, to find her precious house a good owner, to get it in top shape for the transfer and to watch over the details.

And speaking of details, she'd better make a sweep through the house this morning and gather up all the bills, receipts, bank statements and correspondence she could find. Herbert had given her a checklist to start with in searching out Gretta's assets and debts, and the possibilities it enumerated were enough to make Jaymie feel overwhelmed already.

She'd been prepared for the paperwork of paying the last household and hospital bills, but she had no idea if Gretta had owned life insurance or maintained bank accounts outside of Summerset or hidden cash around the house or loaned people money which hadn't been paid back. And the only way to find out, Herbert had said, was to scrutinize every scrap of paper for clues.

Jaymie wished she'd thought to ask Simon some of those questions—though in fact he probably didn't know any more about Gretta's financial affairs than Jaymie did. It wasn't the kind of thing Gretta would be likely to confide in letters or over the telephone, even if Simon had had time to listen.

She wondered what had been so important that he'd had to rush back to Atlanta to take care of it.

The kitchen was as gloomy and gray as the sky outside. That surprised her; Bess should have been downstairs long since, and even if she'd gone back up for something the coffee-pot should be on, and the aroma of her breakfast should be scenting the room. But it looked as if no one had come downstairs yet. Surely Simon wouldn't have commandeered Bess to chauffeur him to the airport?

Jaymie flipped the lights on and surveyed the room, trying to picture it with the changes she was going to make. There was nothing really wrong with the kitchen;

though it had been installed in the thirties, the arrangement was basically good. The painted metal cabinets and stainless-steel counter-tops weren't anywhere close to fashionable these days, but they'd last forever, and even if her budget allowed Jaymie would never consider tearing out something so serviceable—something which, furthermore, fitted the style of the house better than a modern replacement could. But the room could certainly use some softening up. All the metal surfaces, plus the tiled walls, made the place look like an institution. Some new light fixtures would help, but that was beyond her budget for the showcase. She'd have to settle for paint and soft curtains.

Something creaked in the solarium—two rooms away, on the far side of the dining-room—and Jaymie jumped despite herself. It wasn't Bess who had made that noise, for if she'd been in the solarium she'd have heard Jaymie come in and called out a greeting. So perhaps it had just been the house shifting a little—which wasn't exactly a comforting thought, either.

Next you'll be believing in Tommy's ghost, she chided herself, and went looking for Bess. The woman had to be here somewhere. She was probably still upstairs, taking it easy after the stressful events of yesterday.

As she stepped into the dining-room, she heard another creak, this one louder and more distinct, and thought that perhaps Bess had fallen and couldn't call out for help.

She hurried toward the solarium and stopped dead on the threshold at the sight of Simon sprawled across a *chaise-longue*, his face buried against the worn velvet arm. As she watched he rolled over—coming perilously close to sliding off the side of the couch—and fumbled as if reaching for a blanket.

No wonder he was cold, she thought. He was sleeping in his clothes, of course, but he'd discarded his jacket, and the sleeves of his white shirt were rolled up to the elbow. And the room was chilly.

It was also very dim, for the gloomy gray morning light was partly blocked by the old bamboo shades which had been lowered over most of the windows.

Jaymie looked at her wristwatch. It was five minutes past nine. Ten miles out in the countryside, at Summerset Airport, a small commuter airplane had probably just been cleared for takeoff—and Simon was still asleep instead of being on board.

'Well, he can't possibly blame me for this one,' Jaymie muttered. She leaned over him. 'Good morning, Simon.'

He opened his eyes instantly, but he looked at her blankly for a few seconds, as if he couldn't quite focus. There was a red slash down his cheek where it had rested against the decorative braid on the *chaise*. His hair was rumpled, and Jaymie doubted that any steam iron could take the wrinkles out of his shirt.

Then he smiled, and suddenly the overnight growth of beard looked rakishly attractive, and the slash on his cheek took on a romantic air—as if it had been the souvenir of a duel. He raised one hand to stroke her cheek. 'Well, if it isn't Princess Charming,' he murmured. His voice was like warm butterscotch sauce slowly flowing across a dip of ice-cream.

'Come to wake Sleeping Handsome?' Jaymie shook her head. 'Maybe you should look in a mirror.'

'Why? I'd much rather look at you.' His hand slipped to the back of her neck and drew her slowly down toward him.

Jaymie's breath caught in her throat. Surely he didn't intend to kiss her. Didn't they have enough problems without adding that? Maybe he thought he was still asleep, and he was dreaming...

Of me? she thought. Not likely!

Or maybe he always woke up this way and considered any woman within reach fair game. She felt the warmth of his breath against her cheek, and realized that if he pulled her any closer he'd feel the pounding of her heart. And then what might he think? That she was actually attracted to him?

Why shouldn't he think that? she asked herself. She was, wasn't she?

Dammit, Jaymie, she told herself, do something! 'Are you always this romantic in the morning?' She even managed an admiring tone; she had no idea how she pulled it off.

His eyes had drooped, but suddenly she wouldn't bet he was feeling sleepy. 'Always,' he murmured. 'Though I'm even better after a cup of coffee.'

'Well, let me go and I'll make you one.'

Simon grinned at her. 'Want to see what happens?'

Jaymie realized what she'd said and bit her tongue. 'That wasn't... I just meant let me go.'

He showed no signs of hearing her protest. His other hand slipped to the small of her back and tugged her closer.

A note of panic crept into Jaymie's voice. 'I thought you were going to catch the commuter flight.'

'I am.' He blinked and abruptly sat up straight, rubbing the bridge of his nose. 'What time is it, anyway?'

Jaymie almost slid off the side of the *chaise* and had to scramble to catch herself. 'The plane left five minutes ago.' She held out her hand to display her wristwatch.

Simon swore under his breath.

'Why didn't Bess get you up?'

'She's not here. Since I was staying overnight to guard the place, she took advantage of the opportunity to go on to her sister's.'

That was a comfort; Jaymie's fear that Bess was injured or worse had been increasing with every minute the woman didn't appear. 'Some guard you'd be,' she gibed. 'I could have been halfway to Canada with the family treasures before you woke up.'

'What family treasures?' He yawned. 'Has Gretta been holding out on me?'

'Figuratively speaking. What about Herbert? Wasn't he going to drive you to the airport? Or were you so sound asleep he couldn't wake you up?'

'I was going to call him early this morning, so he'd have plenty of time to pick me up.' Simon leaned against the back of the *chaise* and closed his eyes. 'Damn. It must be the gloom, because I'd have sworn it was just past daybreak.'

'It's rotten weather, there's no doubt about that.' Jaymie sat down on the end of the *chaise*, at a safe distance, and drew one booted foot up, clasping her arms around her knee. She glanced at him from the corner of her eye and thanked heaven that he hadn't seemed to notice how she'd been draped over him; he must have still been half asleep after all, despite the sultry line and the smiles...

And you are a fool, Jaymie told herself, to find him attractive when you know darned well what he's like.

Simon stretched and groaned as if every muscle ached.

'Why didn't you at least go upstairs to bed?' she asked.

'I didn't intend to sleep. I just sat down for a minute— between lists——'

'Now don't start trying to blame me. I told you there was no big hurry about those lists.'

'Oh? And just how am I supposed to do them? By memory on the plane? Or do you have a handy-dandy inventory ready for me to take along?'

'Of course not. I just——' She stopped. She suppose she'd expected that he'd come back later, when he could manage it more easily. But obviously he didn't intend to. She wanted to growl; it was going to make her job even tougher if she had to track Simon down in Atlanta to consult him about every decision.

'Anyway,' he said, 'I just sat down for a minute to rest my eyes, and here I am.'

'It's probably Freudian,' Jaymie mused. 'Now that you've spent a few hours in Summerset, you don't want to leave.'

'Are you implying this town's put its hooks into me? I doubt it.' He slid toward the end of the *chaise* and swung his feet down so that he was sitting beside her, one hand braced against the worn velvet upholstery as if he needed all the support he could get. His arm was almost around her. Jaymie sat up a little straighter and eyed him warily.

Simon yawned. 'It's been a rough couple of weeks, and I'm tired out.'

She looked around for somewhere else to sit, but there wasn't a chair in sight, and just standing there would make it obvious that she'd moved to get away from him. 'Lots of overtime at the pizzeria?'

'You can say that again.'

'Well, what are you going to do now that you've missed the plane?'

'Find a cup of coffee, have a shower, and put on a clean shirt.'

'I'll take care of the coffee.' She caught the quick, ironic twinkle in his eyes and knew he'd been awake all the time. A warm rush of color flooded over her and suddenly the room didn't feel chilly any more. Simon started to speak, and Jaymie jumped up. 'For the shower and the shirt, you're strictly on your own.'

Simon followed her to the kitchen and picked up a bag from the counter. 'I was only going to say that I didn't want you to feel it necessary to wait on me,' he said.

Jaymie didn't believe him for an instant, but it was safer to play along. She took a small jar from the refrigerator and measured whole coffee beans into the grinder. 'Oh, that's all right. I want a cup too, and, the condition you're in, you'd probably grind the water and pour the coffee beans into the carafe.' She eyed the bag; it was blazoned with the name of a men's store in the mall, and peeking out the top was a white shirt, still in the package. 'Didn't you even bring an overnight bag?'

'Of course not. I didn't plan to be here overnight.'

She shook her head in disbelief and plugged the coffee-maker in. 'The afternoon commuter doesn't get to St Louis till five, and considering that you'll have a layover of some sort before there's a direct flight to Atlanta...' She reached for a mug and held it in position to catch the fresh stream of coffee.

'Don't remind me. I can't possibly make it home before midnight.'

'On the other hand, you might be in luck.' She slid the glass pot into place and handed Simon the mug.

He inhaled the fragrance and took a long swallow. 'You're driving to St Louis today?' he asked hopefully.

'No, but my friend Holly is. She mentioned it at the meeting last night. She's taking one of her kids to the pediatric orthodontist—but I have to warn you, the child can be a terror.'

'Can't be any worse than some I've run into at the pizza place.' Simon handed her the telephone. 'Get me out of Summerset this morning and I'll be forever grateful, Jaymie.'

She understood his impatience, of course, but she still felt a little flat and resentful at the ripple of eagerness in his voice. 'What's so bad about Summerset, anyway?' she said as she dialed Holly's number. 'It's a nice town.'

Before he could answer, Holly had picked up the phone. She listened patiently to Jaymie's explanation, and then said sweetly, 'I'd be delighted to help out, darling. But I must suggest that you don't tell this story to just everyone.'

Jaymie was honestly at a loss. 'Why?'

'Because they may not believe Simon simply overslept. Everyone who was at the cemetery yesterday saw the sparks flying between the two of you.'

'Believe me, it wasn't that kind of spark!'

Holly laughed and said she'd swing by the Chadwick house in an hour to pick up Simon.

Jaymie hung up the phone, a bit annoyed with herself. Holly suspected romance in the most unlikely of places, so why had Jaymie risen to the bait? 'You've got an hour before Holly comes. Do you want breakfast?' She started to poke around in the freezer. 'Here's a coffee cake Bess must have made. That won't take long to heat.'

'I don't want to keep you from whatever you're supposed to be doing,' he said firmly, and headed for the stairs without waiting for an answer.

Jaymie felt like sticking her tongue out at him. She put the coffee cake in the microwave instead. He might not care if he ate, but she could stand some quick energy.

It was half an hour before he reappeared, and by then the cinnamon aroma of the coffee cake filled the kitchen. He stopped in the doorway with an appreciative sniff.

Jaymie stopped emptying cabinets to take a good look. She felt what was starting to be a familiar tug in the pit of her stomach at the sight of him, and told herself briskly not to be a fool. Yes, the man was good-looking. Any woman with normal inclinations was bound to take a second look—and a third. That didn't mean there was anything serious about the way she reacted to him, for heaven's sake.

Everything considered, she thought, he'd done pretty well. He must have had a razor in that bag of his, too, and with his hair combed and the new shirt he looked quite presentable.

No, that was less than the truth. He looked very good indeed. But she wasn't about to feed the man's ego by telling him. 'Will Bess be coming back this week?'

'I don't think so. I got the impression she wasn't planning to set foot around here till the work was finished. What on earth are you doing?'

'Cleaning all the food out of the cabinets. I intended to tell Bess to take whatever she wanted to her sister's house, but if she's not coming back for a while I guess I'll donate it all to the local food pantry for the needy.' Jaymie dug yet another box of cereal from a dark corner cabinet and wiped the shelf clean. 'Gretta had so much food stored, she could have *been* the local food pantry.'

'But why drag it all out? Stuff like that won't get stale, will it?' Simon cut a couple of wedges from the coffee cake and held one out to Jaymie. 'And nobody on the tour is going to be opening doors and peeking, surely.'

'I hope not. But I have to get the cabinets emptied so I can scrub them down and sand off the paint. The workmen are going to repaint them next week.'

Simon's wedge of coffee cake hung suspended in his hand, obviously forgotten.

Jaymie could almost read his mind. 'I considered painting them brilliant purple,' she said sweetly, 'but on second thought I decided chartreuse with a red stripe would be better.'

'Sounds great to me.'

'It does?'

'All I'd have to do is bring a judge in to see it, and you'd be an ex-executor.'

'I'll keep that in mind.'

'Do,' he said cordially, and munched his coffee cake. 'So what color are you really going to use?'

'Blue-gray. Very neutral, but very warm.'

'Hmm.' Simon shook his head. 'I don't think it will help. Actually, I don't think anything would help this kitchen but a bulldozer, but I'll be happy to look at samples.'

'If you think I'm going to ask your approval of my choices . . .'

'I am, technically, the client, right? So why not humor me?'

'I'm not mailing samples to you in Atlanta, Simon.'

He only smiled. 'You know, it might be kind of fun, having you working for me,' he mused.

Before Jaymie could regain control of her voice, Holly tapped on the back door. 'You know, that driveway really needs widening,' she said when Simon opened it for her. 'Every time I come through the gates, I feel as if I'm going to rip the mirrors off the sides of my van.'

'You shouldn't say that too loudly until someone's bought the house,' Jaymie said. 'You might discourage them.'

'If they drive anything larger than a baby-stroller, they won't need to be told,' Holly said drily. 'But I'll try to keep my observations to myself. The house *is* for sale, then?'

'Not till after the tours are over,' Jaymie said. 'I should introduce you . . .'

'Oh, don't worry about it,' Holly said cheerfully. 'We'll be the best of friends by the time we get to St Louis. Are you ready, Simon?'

'Just let me grab my coat.' Simon was shrugging into his overcoat when he returned to the kitchen, and he came straight across to Jaymie and put both hands on her shoulders. For an incredulous instant she thought he intended to kiss her goodbye, and her traitorous stomach turned a slow, hopeful flip. But he only looked down into her eyes and said, 'I left my lists—what I got done—on Gretta's desk.'

'I'll look them over right now and set things aside.'

'I'll be waiting for the samples.' His voice was so soft, so intimate that he might have been talking of love instead of paint swatches.

Jaymie saw Holly's eyebrows soar and said through gritted teeth, 'Don't hold your breath.'

He smiled and turned toward the door.

A couple of minutes later she heard an engine roar into life, and Holly's van backed slowly from the drive.

Jaymie was standing at the kitchen window, watching. To make sure he's gone, she told herself. And as for the curiously flat feeling that had swept over her—well, that was natural, considering the weight of the responsibility she'd taken on.

It certainly wasn't—it couldn't be—disappointment that Simon had said nothing about ever coming back.

It was incredible how much work could be done in ten short days, Jaymie was thinking as she climbed the back steps of the Chadwick mansion and let herself into the kitchen. The cabinet doors had been sanded, the loose paint removed, and each spot of bare metal splotched with dull gray primer, awaiting the final coat of paint whenever the workmen finally showed up to apply it.

To Jaymie it looked wonderful—almost on schedule and full of promise. Of course, Simon would probably have apoplexy; to inexperienced eyes the place looked as if it was going downhill fast.

She wondered if he'd noticed that there hadn't been any paint samples in his mail. Probably not; no doubt he'd forgotten that nonsense altogether. Jaymie only wished she could. All week, whenever she'd looked at a bit of fabric, she'd found herself wondering what Simon would think of it.

She opened the refrigerator door to put in a container of yoghurt and half a dozen magnets fell off the door.

She patiently picked them up, along with the slips of paper which they'd been holding. The entire front of the refrigerator was covered with notes—questions, comments, complaints, and schedules—and she saw that someone had given up on finding space there and used a felt-tipped marker to leave a message on the stainless-steel counter-top instead.

She hung her coat over the back of a chair and started her regular sweep through the house. She'd check on what had been accomplished since yesterday, and then she'd start stripping wallpaper in the guest room upstairs.

The formal parlor was now painted blue—a startling shade just short of electric. But on one wall, almost hidden behind a door, a silvery glaze had been hand-sponged on a small area, softening the harsh color to a muted, warm glow and giving the whole room a misty, fairy-tale air. It was an old technique with a modern twist, surprisingly well-suited to the house.

Work had scarcely started in the dining-room, but the wallpaper had finally arrived yesterday, so Jaymie would have to catch the decorator soon and find out what she wanted removed from the room before she tackled it...

Her eyes widened in disbelief as she stared at the built-in china cabinets. The shelves were bare, and the doors stood wide open. The contents had been piled haphazardly on the table. At one corner, the depression glass Gretta had collected with such joy was stacked in a wavering pile two feet high. In the middle, a crystal candlestick tottered atop a square pressed-glass cake stand, threatening to fall into a row of water goblets.

If someone came around the corner too fast and bumped into the corner of the table, the dining-room would look as if an earthquake had hit, and all the treasures Gretta had loved and prized would lie in shards on the floor.

Jaymie grabbed for the candlestick and set it safely atop the sideboard. So much for the work she'd planned to do tonight. What had possessed the decorator to drag all of this out without warning?

She went to the solarium for newspapers and a couple of boxes and picked up a notepad from the library. She didn't bother to check the desk drawer where she'd put Simon's lists. They had been short and to the point, and there had been nothing on either one about glassware. She'd have to list each item as she packed it, so that she could give him a description and find out whether he wanted the piece sold or shipped to Atlanta. And whenever he made up his mind she'd have to sort it all out once more.

'And I thought being in charge of the showcase was a big job,' she muttered. 'If I'd known what I was getting into when I agreed to take on Gretta's estate on top of it...'

She'd have done it anyway, and she knew it. There were already passersby stopping at the house, drawn by the sign out front. By the time the House of Dreams officially opened, they'd have people standing in line for tickets. They'd make more money from this than any other fund-raiser in the past ten years.

Holly came in. 'What in heaven's name are you doing? I thought we were going to start stripping wallpaper tonight.'

'You don't think I planned this, do you? Gloria told me she wasn't going to start in here till next weekend. Now I come in and find this mess.'

'I suppose it had to be sorted out sometime.'

'I just hoped I could ask Simon what he wanted before I packed it all up.'

'Why not call him now?'

'I've tried that before. All I get is this sweet-voiced woman——'

'Old? Young?'

'How should I know? She just says politely that she'll give Simon the message, and sure enough within a day or two she calls back and tells me what to do. Only this time I don't have a day or two—this has to be packed up tonight. Would you go get me a couple more empty cartons from the solarium?'

Holly vanished, and Jaymie began gingerly unstacking the more unstable piles of glassware. She didn't look up as footsteps crossed the foyer again, cautiously dodging the piled-up furniture. 'Thanks, Holly. If you'll wrap the depression glass we can get rid of this in a hurry and start on——'

'Just what do you mean, get rid of it, Jaymie?'

Jaymie spun around. Glassware rattled ominously in the air currents created by the heedless movement, but she didn't hear. The cake stand slipped out of her hands.

Simon dived and caught it. Jaymie would have applauded the speed and smoothness of the maneuver if she hadn't been too paralyzed to move.

What was the matter with her anyway? Just minutes ago she'd been complaining about how frustrating it was to deal with him across half the width of the country. Now he was here again, and her first wish had been to wave a hand and send him back to Atlanta. Surely the mere sight of the man shouldn't shake her up like this!

Though she had to admit he looked good. Even better than the last time she'd seen him, that was sure; he looked even taller and leaner in chinos and a sweater, under a leather jacket that had obviously grown buttery soft with age and wear.

He was watching her closely, and there was an ironic gleam in his emerald eyes. 'You were saying, Jaymie?' he prompted.

She swallowed hard. 'The decorator wants to bring in her own accent pieces rather than use Gretta's. So I'm

packing all this up to store—just till you let me know
what you want to keep.'

'I see. Then it's a good thing I decided to come back,
after all.' He set the cake stand down on the sideboard
and smiled at her. 'And how very fortunate it is that this
time I can stay.'

CHAPTER FOUR

'STAY?' Jaymie said weakly. 'For how long?'

Simon's eyes took on a quizzical glow. 'Does this mean you're not looking forward to my company for a while?'

Holly reappeared with a stack of cardboard cartons. 'Well, look who's here! What brings you back to town, Simon?'

'Deadly fear,' he said lightly.

Jaymie wanted to hit him. With all she had done, she thought, it wasn't fair that he still seemed to think she was out to cheat him.

'Of Jaymie, I suppose?' Holly laughed. 'Of course, she *is* such a threatening sort.'

'I'm terrified of what she'll do. I haven't seen a single swatch yet.'

Jaymie said, 'If I give you the whole set, will you go away?' But in the back of her brain something was saying, You're a liar, Jaymie Logan. You're glad to see him.

'And as for having your company,' Jaymie went on crisply, 'now we can really get down to business. You can start by looking through all of this and sorting out what you want to keep and what you don't. Just pack it all up as you go.' She turned on her heel, went directly upstairs to the guest room, and closed the door. She'd have slammed it, but the shock wave reverberating through the house might have been just enough to cause the piles of glassware to crash. Then all Simon would have to do was sweep up the pieces, and if he wasn't busy who knew what he might think of next?

Holly caught up with her a few minutes later, opening the door cautiously, as if she expected tools to come flying at her head.

Jaymie was already on a ladder, holding the portable steamer against the wall. 'This is going to be a mess,' she said. 'There must be ten layers of paper on here, and the steamer doesn't seem to be helping at all.'

'Let me look at it.'

Jaymie handed the appliance down, picked up a scraper, and began impatiently chipping at the wallpaper, scratching a jagged hole in the faded floral pattern. 'See what I mean? It hasn't even soaked through the first layer.'

'That's because the steamer vents are all clogged up with paste.' Holly sat down in the middle of the floor and began poking at the holes which were supposed to funnel steam into the paper. 'It's going to take a while to get this going again, I'm afraid.'

Jaymie growled and got down off the ladder. She filled a bucket in the adjoining bathroom, then picked up a large paintbrush and began slapping hot water directly onto the wallpaper. Rivulets ran down the wall and soaked her arms to the elbow.

'You were certainly curt with Simon,' Holly said. She didn't look up from the steamer.

'At least I wasn't rude.' Jaymie set the bucket down and picked up her scraper again. It skidded across the edge of the wallpaper and gouged a hole in the plaster. 'The man has a nerve, talking about living in deadly fear of me. What does he think I'm trying to do, anyway?' She tossed the scraper aside and picked up the wet paintbrush again with a sigh. 'All I can say is, the next owner had better appreciate all this trouble.'

'Have you had any nibbles on the house?'

'I haven't even listed it yet.'

Holly shrugged. 'I know, but there's always Summerset's grapevine. And it's a great house—I keep waking up at night thinking about it.'

Jaymie laughed. 'Are you sure you're waking up? Maybe you're just having nightmares.'

'No, I mean ... Oh, never mind.'

Jaymie stopped scraping and turned around. 'Are you saying you might really be interested in the house, Holly?'

Holly shrugged. 'I don't know. Maybe you're right and I'm just obsessed because of the showcase. Besides, George would kill me if I told him I wanted to move again.' She held up the steamer. 'Here, try this now.'

An hour later, they were ankle-deep in soggy brown curls of discarded wallpaper when Rob put his head around the corner of the door to study the devastation. 'James, if you don't need anything else moved, I'm going home.'

'Come in for a minute and I'll sweep up some of this garbage for you to carry out.'

Reluctantly, Rob stepped into the mess. 'Whew, you've certainly got it hot enough in here.' He picked up a trash bag and held it open for Jaymie to fill. 'Hey, I like Simon, by the way.'

'Oh? You've been talking to him instead of working?'

'Of course not. I've been helping him pack up your glass stuff in the dining-room.'

'*My* glass?' Jaymie stopped sweeping and stared at him. 'Is that what he said it was?'

Rob shrugged. 'Not exactly, I guess. Just something about you telling him to do it. I told him not to let it bother him, because you get on these bossy streaks every now and then.'

'Thanks a bunch, Rob.' Jaymie tied the top of the black plastic bag and handed it to him. 'Put this by the garbage cans out back, and I'll see you after school tomorrow.'

Holly went home a little later, but Jaymie, remembering how little time there was and how much remained to be done, kept on. There was a steady pattern to the work—the gentle hiss of steam, the rhythmic scratching of the scraper, the soft patter of discarded wallpaper falling into piles at her feet. The repetitive motion, coupled with the warm humidity of the room, conspired to make Jaymie sleepy. She missed Holly's cheerful chatter, too.

After a while she put the steamer down and curled up on the corner of the brass daybed, the only piece of furniture still in the room. It was draped with a plastic sheet, so it wasn't the most comfortable perch in the world. But she didn't care. She'd just sit and rest for a minute, then go down and get her yoghurt—it wasn't much of a dinner, but for tonight it would have to do—and she'd work a little longer...

The door wasn't latched, and she didn't hear it open till Simon said cheerfully, 'I thought everyone had gone home and left the lights on. Do you know what time it is?'

Jaymie twisted around. 'About ten, I expect. Why?'

'Try fifteen minutes past midnight.'

'Really? How time flies when you're having fun.'

He sat down beside her and popped the top on his soda can. 'Want this? I'll go get another.'

'Maybe a sip. There should be a glass in the bathroom.'

He came back with a paper cup, filled it to the rim, and ceremonially raised the can in a wordless toast. 'Why are you stripping the wallpaper?'

'Because if you put new paper on the wall over it and the old glue fails, it all falls off and you've got a king-sized mess.'

Simon looked at the half-scraped wall and the mass of crumpled brown fragments on the floor. 'It doesn't appear likely to fail,' he said mildly. 'That stuff looks as if it's hanging on for dear life.'

'Today's adhesives sometimes react in unexpected ways with old paper and glue.'

'Oh. Well, at any rate, that wasn't exactly what I meant. Why are you, personally, stripping wallpaper?'

Jaymie sighed. 'Because designer showcases are expensive projects all the way around. If I do the work myself at least I'm not out of pocket for workmen's wages.'

'And that explains your little brother, too, I suppose. He seems a nice kid.'

'Don't give Rob credit for volunteering his time,' Jaymie muttered. 'You wouldn't believe the size of the car repair bill I paid last week. It would take him months to work that off.' She crumpled the empty paper cup and cast a longing look at his soda can. 'You know, if you wouldn't mind——'

'You'd like one after all?'

'Yes. And would you bring up my yoghurt and the package of bagels? I'll share.'

He reappeared a couple of minutes later with a small tray. 'By the way, if that's the color the cabinets are going to end up, Jaymie, you can stop bragging about how much you're improving this house.'

'It's not. That's just the primer.'

He frowned. 'I thought you said they'd be painted by now.'

Jaymie couldn't remember. 'Contractors. You know what they're like. Or maybe—if you're lucky—you don't.'

'You amaze me. You're not painting them yourself?'

'I probably would, but it takes a special kind of spray paint and——'

'*Spray paint*?'

'Don't try to make it sound like I'm turning kids loose with aerosol cans. It's a commercial outfit which specializes in this kind of thing.'

Simon didn't look convinced. 'The place already looks like the underside of a bridge.'

'I suppose you mean the message scribbled on the counter-top?'

'What's next? Graffiti on the front door?'

'Why are you so worried, Simon? It'll look good. Even if it doesn't, you'll stand to lose a little money, I suppose, but I could lose my reputation. And in my business, where image is everything, that matters.' She finished her yoghurt and tossed the empty container into a nearby garbage bag. 'Want a bagel?'

'Sure.' Simon sat down on the edge of the daybed. 'How much money are you going to have invested in this project by the time it's done?'

Jaymie shook her head. 'I don't want to think about how far I'm probably over budget. I'll add the figures up after it's finished and remind myself that I'll get it all back eventually in advertising value.' She slid off the daybed and reached for the steamer. She might as well be accomplishing something.

Simon settled himself more comfortably and reached for a bagel. He looked as if he was making himself at home. Surely, at midnight, after a long trip, he should be interested in a good night's sleep. 'Where are you staying, Simon?'

He broke a bite-sized chunk from his bagel. 'Here.'

'What do you mean, *here*?' Jaymie sputtered. 'There's no place for you.'

'Yes, I noticed that even the *chaise-longue* is gone. Did you do that on purpose?'

'Of course not. It's being re-upholstered.'

'And re-sprung, one hopes,' Simon murmured. 'The underlying support was certainly in need of attention.'

'You can't sleep in the solarium, anyway. There aren't any shades at the moment.'

'That wouldn't be my first choice, no.'

'There's a hotel downtown. It's not deluxe, but it's not expensive either.'

Simon considered, and shook his head. 'No, I think I'd rather stay closer to the action. Will you be taking tours into the tower room?'

'No,' Jaymie said reluctantly. 'But that doesn't mean——'

'I'll just throw a sleeping-bag on the floor. Look at the positive side, Jaymie. I'll be out of everyone's way up there, and you'll have a nightwatchman on duty.'

'Some watchman,' Jaymie muttered. 'The way you sleep, someone could steal the whole first floor out from under you and you'd never notice.'

'Now that's not fair,' he protested. 'I explained that I was completely exhausted that night. Oversleeping isn't my normal behavior.'

And what about the way he'd awakened that morning? Was that normal—the sultry voice and the sensual behavior? Forget it, Jaymie, she told herself. It's not good for you to remember that.

'Look, Simon...' She met his gaze and paused at the gleam of detached interest she saw there. He wasn't at all worried about her answer, she realized. In fact, there was a sparkle of humor in his eyes—as if he expected that she'd try to throw him out, and was looking forward to it, knowing that he'd win in the end.

Technically, of course, even though he was the heir he couldn't take full possession of the house till the estate was settled. And, since Simon had announced his wish to sell it, she didn't think he had any legal right to move in.

But, as a practical matter, she couldn't evict him. Till a sale was final, the house was part of his inheritance. And in a town like Summerset, where most business was done on a handshake and detailed legalities were eyed with suspicion, Jaymie would look like a fool if she tried to keep Simon out.

So she settled for a warning. 'The tower room isn't heated. You'll be awfully uncomfortable up there.'

'I'll leave the door open at the foot of the steps.'

'With all the traffic through the house every day, this isn't going to be a restful vacation. Some of the contractors start work at six in the morning.'

He nodded. 'The next thing you'll do, no doubt, is remind me that Gretta was going to move out for the duration.'

'And that's exactly why—the noise, dust, discomfort and confusion. She'd have been here every day watching the work, I'm sure, but she couldn't have been comfortable trying to live here. If one can't sleep well at night——'

'I can appreciate that it may be a problem.' Simon's tone was innocent. 'And if you're offering me the same deal you were going to give Gretta . . .'

Jaymie took her eyes off the wallpaper and gouged a chunk out of the plaster. 'You mean, move in with me?' Her voice was little more than a squeak.

'What a lovely idea! I'm very grateful to you for thinking of my comfort and well-being, and I——'

Jaymie's face flamed. 'Of course I'm not suggesting you move in with me!'

'That's what I figured,' Simon said crisply. 'So I'll stay here and pretend I'm camping out. Surely you don't have any real objection. Since Gretta's estate is paying the utilities at the moment——'

'Actually, it's not; the Service League is. But of course it's up to you. If you really want to play nightwatchman for a while ... Why *are* you here, anyway? A couple of weeks ago the pizza place was keeping you so busy you could hardly get away overnight.'

'Oh, that.' Simon dismissed the question with a casual wave of his hand. 'The business was bought out, and they didn't need me any more, so I'm footloose at the moment.'

Jaymie stared at him, eyes narrowed. It wouldn't be the first time, of course, that a good employee had been thrown out of work through no fault of his own. On the other hand, there could be any number of other reasons for Simon's being abruptly unemployed, and most of them weren't nearly so innocent. 'There's a fishy sort of aroma about you, Simon.'

'That would be the anchovies, no doubt. We use a fair amount of them in the pizza business. It's always a problem, because they have such a distinctive smell, and it clings forever.'

'I meant the story, not you personally.' As a matter of fact, Simon himself smelled faintly of aftershave. Jaymie couldn't identify the brand, though the musky scent was vaguely familiar. Or did she just remember it from that morning on the *chaise-longue* when he'd almost kissed her? That must be it; she remembered everything else about that morning, far better than she wanted to.

'Not many people like anchovies,' Simon went on, 'but the ones who do are really devoted.'

Jaymie gave up. Simon's employment wasn't any of her business. 'I suppose you'd like to start drawing funds from the estate? I'll do the best I can, but there isn't a lot of loose cash in Gretta's accounts. She seems to have drained everything to fund the pension for Bess.'

'Oh, I can hold out for a little while.'

'Well, I'm sorry you're at loose ends.'

'Are you? I'm not. I was getting awfully itchy to see what on earth you were doing.'

Jaymie lost her temper. 'You can't be serious about the paint samples, can you? Look, Simon, there's nothing more I could do to keep you informed. I've called you on every damned detail, whether I was obligated to or not——'

'I know. That's why I was getting itchy. If you didn't have anything better to do than bug me every time you wanted to toss out a broken cup, it made me wonder if anything important was getting done. And frankly, now that I've seen the place——'

'All right, so you still have to use a little imagination. It'll be great in a couple of weeks.' She shut off the steamer and wondered how long it would take to cool. She couldn't go home for the night till it was cleaned. If she'd had any sense at all, she'd have quit when Holly did and avoided this argument, too.

A muscle in her forearm complained as she set the steamer down, and she winced and rubbed it.

'What's the problem?' Simon said.

'I've pulled something somehow. It's all this repetitive motion, I suppose.'

'Let me see.'

'There's nothing to look at, Simon.'

But Simon had already taken her hand and pushed her cuff up. His fingers were warm and strong against the tired muscles of her forearm, stroking and massaging, and tingles began to race from her wrist to elbow and beyond. 'Come and sit down,' he ordered.

'Simon...' But she perched on the corner of the daybed next to him.

His thumbs dug gently into the delicate bones of her wrists, and Jaymie shivered. 'Does that hurt?' He was looking at her face, not her hands.

'Hurt, no. But the pressure——'

'That's just working the built-up stress out of your body. Lean back and relax.' He held her wrist steady with one hand, while the other rubbed her palm. 'Do you have any idea how many muscles there are in your hands? When you hold them in one position for hours, it's no wonder you get cramps and pains. Every kink needs to be worked out, one by one.'

His voice was almost hypnotic. Jaymie closed her eyes. She had never thought about her hand as anything but a single entity, but as Simon massaged she could actually feel separate muscles stretching, loosening and relaxing. He went on to each finger, rubbing and tugging.

When he started on her other hand, Jaymie said unsteadily, 'How many muscles did you say there are in my hands?'

Simon smiled a little. 'I haven't the faintest idea.'

'But you said——' Jaymie opened her eyes. 'Oh, I know, you just like to play with hands.'

He was silent for a moment, while he rubbed the last finger and folded it gently back into her palm. 'Some hands, at any rate,' he admitted. He hadn't released her wrist, and he'd leaned so close that his breath stirred a tendril of hair on her forehead.

He was going to kiss her. Not a good idea, Jaymie thought hazily, though at the moment she wasn't quite sure why she was hesitating. The prospect was every bit as inviting as it had been that morning in the solarium...

Simon leaned even closer. There was a soft glow in the depths of his eyes. Jaymie moved a little, and the plastic drape which covered the daybed shifted abruptly and slid her to the very edge. She clutched at Simon; his arm came round her like a barricade to keep her from falling, and suddenly she was half lying on the daybed with him bending over her—the most vulnerable position she could imagine.

'It's late,' she said unsteadily. 'I'd better go home.'

For a moment she thought he hadn't heard her. His lips brushed her temple, seeming to scorch the soft skin, and she sighed a little and turned her head, seeking his mouth.

His kiss was even more gentle than she had expected, but there was no hesitation in it, no pleading, no questioning. He had too much self-confidence for that, and she wondered if he'd developed it by kissing other women, or if it simply was part of everything he did. Then, as his obvious pleasure sparked a rising desire in her, she forgot all about it and only sought to hold him close.

'Perhaps you're right,' he murmured finally.

Jaymie looked up at him in confusion.

'About going home,' he added softly. Her face flamed, and he watched the color come and go with evident enjoyment. 'You see, Jaymie, I'd hate it if you didn't still respect me in the morning.'

Jaymie didn't get back to the Chadwick house till noon the following day. The rooms were quiet, for the workers had all left for lunch. Simon was nowhere to be seen, either, but the mess in the dining-room had been reduced to a dozen boxes. She poked through a couple of them; though she didn't want to admit it, she was curious about his taste. She told herself hers was a reasonable interest, because if she understood the kind of thing he cared about she wouldn't have to consult him about every decision.

And, despite what he had said last night about staying in Summerset for a while, she didn't think it was likely that he'd be around long. He didn't appear to have an excess of cash, or surely he'd have checked in at the hotel instead of camping out in the tower room. And he wasn't going to be getting much money from Gretta's estate for a while; she couldn't give him what simply wasn't there.

Jaymie supposed she should list the house right away and get the process in motion.

She didn't want to, of course. Putting a house up for sale in the condition this one was in would be inviting trouble; even truly interested buyers couldn't help but be put off by this distracting mess. But if she asked the realtor not to advertise it yet and to show it cautiously... It was the best compromise Jaymie could come up with.

Digging through the boxes Simon had packed was a waste of time, since none of them seemed to be marked. Were these things the treasures he wanted to keep, or the junk he intended to get rid of? Nothing appeared to be packed well enough for a trip across country, that was certain.

The back door banged and she jumped and closed the top of a box. Simon was in the kitchen unloading a grocery bag when she came in. A few frozen dinners, a couple of cans of beef stew—— But itemizing his purchases was not helping her ignore her faster than normal heartbeat. What an idiot she was, she thought. Just because the man had kissed her last night it was no reason to panic at seeing him today. Especially since it hadn't seemed to be anything out of the ordinary to him. Oh, he'd enjoyed himself; she didn't have any doubt about that. But that crack about wanting her still to respect him in the morning... Obviously Simon hadn't been anywhere close to losing his head, and she was more than a little embarrassed to have to admit that she had.

It wasn't fair, she thought. Fully half the time she didn't even like the man, so why should she turn to cinders the moment he touched her?

'Decided to stay?' Jaymie said. She sounded a little breathless, but maybe if she was lucky he wouldn't notice.

He stopped unloading the bag and turned to look at her with a half-smile which tugged at her throat. 'Unless you're going to make me a better offer.'

'Of course not. I respect you too much.'

'I knew I'd regret saying that,' Simon muttered. 'Of course, it wouldn't take much to be a better offer. My neck is twisted into the shape of a question mark after a night in that room.'

'Oh? Wasn't camping out as charming as you thought? You can't say I didn't warn you that you weren't likely to be comfortable up there.'

'No, but you could have been more specific. You could have told me, for instance, that the open space in the tower room is now less than three feet square because the rest of the floor has been stacked with discards from the rest of the house.'

'Honestly? I haven't been up there lately. But there wasn't anything else we could do with all the furniture,' she pointed out. 'The basement's too damp to store anything down there.'

'The basement's damp too? The roof leaks, the kitchen has—count 'em—two electrical outlets, the bathrooms are prehistoric, and now you tell me the basement's damp? Are you sure *anybody's* going to want this house?'

'This is a great house.'

Simon's eyes narrowed. 'Right. And Attila the Hun was a nice neighbor, too. Why are you storing stuff, anyway? Haven't you considered getting rid of it? I know there are things up there you've asked me about.'

'You see, the trouble with most of Gretta's things is they're not old enough to be considered antiques and not new enough to have much resale value.'

'What's that got to do with anything?'

'The best way to dispose of stuff like that is an auction. A big, day-long auction—but only one. Which means waiting till everything's sorted out. So whenever you said you didn't want something I——'

He growled, 'You shoved it up in the tower till auction day. Dammit, Jaymie——'

'Well, how was I to know you'd end up there?' Jaymie asked reasonably.

Simon rubbed the nape of his neck as if it hurt. 'Aren't there auction places that take things on consignment and have regular sales? At least then it would be out of the house.'

'Yes, there are—but you're in the Midwest, Simon. You'll get more out of the merchandise by holding the auction here, right on the grounds. People will make a day of it, and if auction fever takes hold they'll pay ridiculous prices for ordinary things just because they were part of the Chadwick estate.'

'My vertebrae are worth something too.'

Jaymie shrugged. 'I suppose it's up to you. I'll give you the names of the consignment places. But I think you'd be better off in the long run if you commandeered Rob this afternoon to shove some boxes around up in the tower and make some room. Then you can take the daybed out of the guest room and haul it upstairs.'

'How you think moving a few boxes will make enough room for a daybed... Aren't you going to use it?'

'When the showcase opens, yes, but I won't need it back for a week or so.'

'Oh, that's a comfort,' Simon mocked.

So he intended to stay at least a week. 'Take it or leave it,' Jaymie said, and climbed the stairs to tackle the wallpaper again. She spent the first half-hour cleaning the dried paste out of the steamer, feeling grateful that Holly wasn't around to ask why she'd neglected to clean it last night.

She was just getting into the rhythm of the job once more when Rob came in. 'James, about those boxes of stuff in the dining-room,' he began.

'Check with Simon about what he wants to keep.'

'None of it, he says.'

'*None*? Doesn't the man have any taste at all?'

Simon appeared around the door. 'Only bad, obviously,' he said calmly. He picked up a scraper and began to score wallpaper.

Jaymie bit her lip. 'I'm sorry. That was very rude.'

'So shall I put it all in the tower room?' Rob asked.

Jaymie glanced at the daybed and tried to calculate the number of boxes she'd already consigned to the tower room. Then there were the things Gretta had stashed up there through the years, crates that Jaymie had deliberately postponed opening until the showcase was finished and the auction could be arranged. Considering what Simon had said, the place must already be stacked to the ceiling.

'I don't know where to put it,' she admitted. 'Let me think. In the meantime you can start tearing the daybed apart.'

'To haul it upstairs, you mean?' Rob said. 'We don't need to. Simon and I figured it all out.'

'Oh, I can't wait to hear this one,' Jaymie said under her breath.

Rob grinned. 'I called Mom, and she invited him to stay with us as long as he wants. He's going to have your old room, James.'

Jaymie gasped. 'Simon, you can't possibly move in with my parents! You've never even met them!'

'Come on, James,' Rob scoffed. 'Mom and Dad have never in their lives minded when we brought somebody home. They've always said they want to meet our friends.'

'Meeting is one thing, moving in's another. Besides, in the circumstances, I have trouble believing that Mom and Dad accepted Simon as a bosom buddy of yours, Rob.'

'Oh, I didn't say he was,' Rob said cheerfully. 'I told them it was all your idea.'

CHAPTER FIVE

'IF YOU don't need me any more just now,' Rob added, 'I'll be in the kitchen.' With a casual wave, he vanished down the stairs.

'Checking out whether someone brought cookies, no doubt.' Simon put his scraper down and looked around as if he was searching for something.

'I should have smothered him the day Mom brought him home from the hospital,' Jaymie muttered. 'That's when the idea first occurred to me, but I was only four and I thought things might improve. If I'd realized...'

'Oh, I don't know. He seems a pretty good kid to me.'

Jaymie glared at him. 'But then, you're prejudiced at the moment, aren't you? Wait till you get to know him better.'

'I'll have every opportunity, won't I? How about if I run the steamer and you scrape?' He picked up the steamer.

'I thought you were just playing. You're actually going to help?'

'Well, it's a bit boring just to watch, and obviously you can use all the help you can get. How does this thing work, anyway?'

Jaymie took the steamer out of his hands and demonstrated. Simon watched for a couple of minutes, then he took the appliance back and held it against the wallpaper at shoulder level. 'No wonder your arms hurt last night from holding this thing up. It's an awkward angle.'

'Lean into it a little.' Jaymie picked up the scraper again. She would have to stay close to Simon so that she could remove each swatch of wallpaper as soon as he slid the steamer to the next little patch, before the old paste had a chance to cool and harden once more. It was not only an awkward angle, she soon realized, but an awkward position as well. At times, Simon practically had his arms around her. Why hadn't she thought of that before she agreed to this cooperative effort?

Because down deep you kind of like the idea, she admitted. And as long as he was offering to take a turn—well, he was right. She could use all the help she could get.

Simon smelled of aftershave again today, mixed with the pleasant tang of soap. Jaymie still couldn't quite recognize the scent, and a little later she found herself taking deep breaths as she tried to identify the brand. She was thoroughly embarrassed at catching herself in such a silly effort, but at least Simon hadn't seemed to notice.

Rob came in a little later with an enormous hunk of chocolate cake in one hand. 'I forgot to tell you, James. Mom said you're to come to dinner tonight, too, to help make Simon feel at home his first night.' He eyed the two of them, working on a single square foot of wallpaper, and then glanced around at the other three walls, which were still almost untouched. 'Though Mom's definition of "at home" might not be quite what you have in mind.'

Jaymie glared at him.

Rob said hastily, 'I think I'd better go see if I can't help out downstairs.' Then he poked his head back in and added, 'Shall I put a "Do Not Disturb" sign on this door?'

Jaymie drew back her arm and took aim with her scraper, and Rob grinned and vanished.

'You're lucky, you know,' Simon said. 'Having a brother, I mean.'

'One like *Rob*? You must be joking.'

'Not at all. I'm speaking from the perspective of an only child, you understand.'

'You'd soon change your mind if you had to put up with him all the time. And, come to think of it, starting tonight you will. What a lovely thought!'

Simon smiled. 'You're making me wonder if I've been wrong all these years.'

Jaymie stopped scraping and looked him over speculatively. 'Let me know what you think in a few days. If you like the idea, I'll make you an unconditional gift of Rob, and maybe I can find out what it's like to be an only child.'

'He told me you used to make him play house with you.'

'It was one way to get rid of him, you see,' Jaymie explained. 'I'd let him be the daddy, and I'd send him off to work. Unfortunately he caught on by the time he was six and after that he was just a sheer pain in the neck.'

He angled a look down at her. 'Why do I suspect you're a great deal fonder of him than you'll admit?'

'Watch out, Simon. You'll make me start thinking you're a romantic.'

He smiled a little. 'Have you always liked to play house?'

'Are you implying I've never outgrown it?'

'Well,' he said reasonably, 'it doesn't look as if you have. Tell me what you're going to do with this room.'

'Very simple, sunny and bright. Nothing too fussy, because guests are easily put off by rooms that are too elaborate. Lace bedspreads are pretty, for instance, but they're terrifying to people who aren't used to them.' She glanced up at him. 'Let me put your mind at rest— you won't have that sort of problem at my parents' house. When Rob said you were getting my old room, that's literally what he meant. Not a thing's been done to it since the day I moved out.'

'You amaze me, Jaymie. I thought you were a real interior decorator.'

She smiled a little. 'I'm a practical one. I tried to convince Mom once to let me turn it into an office for her, but she pointed out that I'd have to remove all the junk I left there, so I stopped nagging her about it.'

Simon's eyes brightened. 'Junk? Do you mean things like your dolls and stuffed toys and school papers? This might be even more fun than I thought.'

'Don't get your hopes up. I was very careful not to leave any old love letters lying about.'

'I'd have been disappointed if you had. You strike me as a much more cautious sort than that. Tell me what you do when you're not working on houses.'

'It seems so long since I've had any free time that I've forgotten what I used to do with it.' They'd almost reached the corner, and in that confined space she was terribly aware of Simon's closeness and the warmth of the room. 'I seem to have vague memories of long walks with Rob's Irish setter, and basketball games——'

'You play?'

'No, but I'm a great cheering section for the home team. And once upon a time I played the piccolo in the local symphony.'

Simon shifted the steamer to his other hand and rested his forearm on Jaymie's shoulder for a few seconds. 'This thing gets heavy after a while.'

His arm was almost encircling her, and his breath stirred the hair at her temple. Jaymie felt as if all the air had been sucked from her lungs. 'Want to trade jobs?' she managed to say.

'And ruin my macho image? Of course not. Are you having trouble breathing?' he asked helpfully. 'The atmosphere *is* a little heavy in here. Maybe we should take a break.'

And afterwards she'd find a way to work across the room from him, Jaymie thought. But as she looked up at him to agree she saw the mischief dancing in his eyes. He knew exactly why she was breathless, and Jaymie was darned if she'd give him extra satisfaction by admitting it. She raised her chin a bit and said, 'It's just the humidity from the steamer, and it'll really start loosening the paper now.'

'Whatever you say,' he murmured.

They worked in silence for a couple of minutes. 'You're not bad at this, you know,' Jaymie said finally.

'I'm a fast learner.'

'Have you always been in pizza?'

'Oh, no. Before pizza it was radio, and before that——'

'Radio?'

'You sound surprised.'

'Not really, I suppose. With your voice, you'd be a natural.' It was just that it didn't seem to fit. Television seemed more likely, somehow.

'Do you like it?'

'Your voice?' If he thought she was going to admit that listening to him read the telephone book would make her bones melt, he was wrong. 'It's very nice.' Hastily, before he could pursue that, she added, 'And what's next? After pizza?'

'At the moment, I'm not quite sure. But I'll know it when it comes along,' he said blithely. 'Maybe now that I know how to take wallpaper off, I'll learn how to put it on, and you can hire me.'

'I've got a good wallpaper-hanger already. Besides, it's not as easy as it looks to hang stripes and get them straight, you know.'

The news didn't seem to crush him. 'Is that what you're using in here?'

Jaymie nodded. 'Yellow and white stripes. The whole room is based on a watercolor painting I'm borrowing from the gallery down in the mall.'

'They'll let you do that?'

Jaymie nodded. 'The pamphlets will give credit to the gallery and the artist, and I'd be amazed if the painting doesn't sell before the tours are over. It's a great deal for everyone.'

'What's so special about the painting?'

'It's a view of three little kids in yellow slickers playing marbles in the rain. As soon as I saw that watercolor, this room came into focus in my mind—the striped wallpaper representing the rain, and a floral border right above the baseboard to portray the garden the kids are playing in——'

'You make the whole room sound like a painting.'

Jaymie glanced up at him doubtfully, wondering if he was making fun of her. Perhaps it did sound silly, but that was the way she worked—just as an artist balanced shapes and colors and symbolic elements to create the image of a three-dimensional world on a flat canvas.

But he seemed serious enough, for a change.

'It's sort of like that,' she said. 'The quilt is a simple pattern of interlocking circles in yellow and white, and——'

'Like puddles?'

She was startled. 'As a matter of fact, I hadn't thought of that. The members of Mother's church group made the quilt—they're going to sell raffle tickets on it during the tours. So I just told them the colors, and they chose the pattern.'

'I'm terribly disappointed in you, Jaymie.'

'Well, it isn't as if there can only be one right choice. I was never the sort of decorator who insisted that once

a room was finished nothing could ever be moved again.'
She shifted her scraper to the other hand and flexed her
fingers to relieve a cramp in her wrist. 'Then I'll add
throw-pillows in primary colors—the painting has
touches of red and blue and green. And on the mantel
I'm going to put a big glass jar of marbles.'

Simon said thoughtfully, 'What will happen to the
room when someone buys the painting?'

'Oh, we won't let the watercolor go till the showcase
closes down. Besides, maybe the people who buy the
house will get the painting too. Prospective buyers will
see everything in place, and who knows? They might
want to keep it that way.'

'Anything's possible,' Simon conceded. 'Who do you
think will end up living here, Jaymie?'

She looked up at him in surprise. Was the question
purely curiosity, or did he really care? 'Holly, maybe.
She said she might be interested.'

His eyebrows quirked, but he didn't comment.

'But whoever it is I hope it's someone who loves the
house, not only the structure but the history of it.
Someone who'll make it the center of Summerset's
culture again. Someone who'll raise a family here, and
pass the love and the heritage on to another generation.'
Her voice was soft, almost husky, and she had to clear
her throat before she could go on. 'That's what Gretta
wanted too, I'm sure. Remember what I said about her
will—that she might have had a premonition? The more
I think about it, the more certain I am that she somehow
knew she wasn't going to see this project finished.'

'What makes you say that?'

'Because the whole idea behind it was her suggestion.
Not the showcase itself, I mean—I'm the one who came
up with that. But once the decision was made Gretta
really threw herself into it. That's one reason I want so
much for this to be a success—because she wanted it so

badly. She's the one who created the Ideal Family. She always said it that very precise way, too, as if it should be capitalized.'

He frowned. 'The Ideal Family? I don't quite know what you're getting at.'

'We were walking through the house one day, sharing ideas, and suddenly she said, "This room should be the nursery."'

'What?' He sounded startled.

Jaymie laughed. 'I know what you mean. I thought I was hallucinating—after all, Gretta and babies aren't the most likely combination in the world.'

Simon nodded in agreement.

'Then she laughed at my expression and said it would be silly to decorate this house for her, that it would make a dull tour because there wouldn't be enough variety from room to room. She wanted it to reflect a family, but since we didn't have a real family she thought we should imagine one, like a happily-ever-after fairy-tale. And so that's what we're doing—designing the house to fit Gretta's Ideal Family.'

'And I'm sure she told you all about it.' His drawl had somehow grown slower, richer—and full of irony.

Jaymie felt herself coloring a little. How had she gotten herself into this, anyway? The Ideal Family had sounded terribly reasonable when Gretta had described it, but repeating the details to Simon was a different thing altogether. How had she managed to forget that he wasn't the type to appreciate Gretta's brand of romance?

But it was too late to back out; she'd have to finish. 'The Ideal Couple are very much in love with each other,' she began, 'despite having been married long enough to have the proverbial two kids, dog, cat, and station wagon. The Ideal Man is a professional, Gretta said——'

'I suppose she had his job mapped out, too?'

'Not exactly. She just said he isn't so devoted to his work that he can't enjoy his family and his home and his hobbies.' She laughed a little, remembering some of the things Gretta had said. 'She had all sorts of fun with that—imagining him building birdhouses in the basement. Oh, and she even said once that he was the kind who played the violin—not terribly well, but enthusiastically. And she——'

Simon was looking at her quizzically. 'Are you talking about Gretta? Or do you mean the Ideal Woman?'

'Sorry. I am getting tripped up in pronouns, aren't I? At the moment the Ideal Woman—though she's involved in civic affairs—is mainly a stay-at-home mom who enjoys her kids. She's the kind of woman who keeps a rocking chair in the kitchen so she's always ready to read a story. And at the end of the day, after the kids are bathed and in bed, and the Ideal Couple retreat to their own bedroom...' She noticed that Simon was giving her a very quizzical look, and she stopped abruptly, feeling warm confusion radiating from the pit of her stomach till her whole body was tingling with the sensation. 'Don't look at me like that. I'm giving you *Gretta's* description, you understand.'

'Of course,' he murmured. 'How did you decide who decorates which rooms?'

Jaymie tried not to sigh in relief at being taken away from the subject of the Ideal Family. Why had she allowed her tongue to run away with her, anyhow? As if Simon cared about Gretta's fantasies! 'We drew lots.'

'And your share was the guest room and the kitchen?' He sounded dubious. 'That hardly seems a fair distribution.'

Jaymie shrugged. 'I'm doing the library too. And I didn't get stuck with the kitchen, I volunteered for it.'

'For Gretta's sake,' he said softly. It was not a question.

Jaymie nodded. 'I was afraid somebody else would give it a slapdash job. And Gretta was so excited about all the ideas ... I wish she could see how the house is turning out.' Her eyes were stinging a little.

Simon turned away to refill the steamer. Jaymie was glad; it gave her a moment to get her composure back. She tugged at a loose seam under the window and was startled when a big chunk of plaster fell at her feet with a crash.

Simon turned around to survey the damage. 'Nice job, Jaymie.'

'I didn't break it. It was already loose.'

'It looks as if the house has shifted. There are cracks all over the place.'

'It's settled, no doubt. All houses settle, and this one's over a hundred years old, so it's got a right.'

'Have you ever considered that maybe it's not worth the effort?'

'Of course not. Why are you so gloomy about this house, anyway?'

'Because I don't want to get my hopes too high for what this place is going to end up looking like. Take the living-room, for instance——'

'What about it?'

'The damned thing's blue. And not *just* blue, it's *overwhelmingly* blue.'

'It won't stay that way. It's going to have a nice soft silvery glaze, and you'll hardly see the underlying color.'

Simon gave her a dubious look. 'Personally, I don't see the point in putting it there and then covering it up, but if you say so ... What about that contraption in the room across the hall?'

'The Ideal Child's room? It's a loft bed.'

'Really? I've never seen anything quite like it.'

'I'm not surprised. Actually, it's the front porch off an old house, and the mattress goes on top of it. Just think about it, Simon. Any child would love it—it's like having a tree house right in his room.'

'You sound as if it was your idea.'

'It was,' she admitted. 'The decorator was going to put up pink flowered wallpaper. It was very nice wallpaper, but the Ideal Child wouldn't have liked it at all.'

He lifted one eyebrow as if to ask how she could possibly know for sure what an imaginary child would care for.

'Oh, I know,' Jaymie said. 'Why make all the fuss about the Ideal Family?'

'The question had crossed my mind,' Simon said drily.

'Because it mattered to Gretta. Besides, a good decorator studies her clients. She doesn't force her own taste on everyone else. If I approached a house blindly, every one I worked on would look like all the rest, and ultimately they'd all be ordinary—no personality at all.'

Simon smiled a little. 'I suspect nothing you ever did could be considered ordinary, Jaymie.'

She couldn't quite decide if that was a compliment or not. She only knew her pulse-rate was reacting as if it was.

'Have you been studying me?' His voice was satin-smooth.

Jaymie felt just a tinge of panic. What kind of question was that? 'Why would I?'

'Officially, I'm your client, Jaymie. So what do you have in mind for me?'

She laughed in relief. 'Sorry. The Ideal Family has priority just now. You might do me a favor, by the way, and start going through the books in the library to choose what you want to keep.'

'There must be thousands of them.'

'Exactly. I can't do it, because I don't know your taste in literature. And it would be a great time to get it out of the way, since Rob took all the books down so we could polish the shelves. I don't think it had been done in decades—you wouldn't believe the dust we found up there.'

'In that case, I doubt there are any books I'm longing to read, either.'

Jaymie eyed him in disbelief.

'You're disappointed in me?' Simon guessed.

'Are you certain you're really Gretta's nephew? Maybe you're adopted.'

'Nope. See this? It's the Chadwick chin.' He tapped the cleft.

'Are you positive of that?' Jaymie said doubtfully. 'Gretta didn't have a dimple.'

'It's not a dimple. And it seems to be like baldness—it's passed on by women, but shows up only in men. Check out the family pictures.'

'I will. But I'm still not going to be convinced that you're truly a Chadwick. Don't you have any family feeling at all?'

'If you define family feeling as wanting to hang onto every dish or printed page or piece of cloth that ever belonged to someone called Chadwick, no. And don't act so surprised. This isn't my ancestral home, you know.'

'But your mother grew up here. She was Gretta's sister.'

Simon shook his head. 'They were half-sisters. My mother was born of the first marriage, and she was only a baby when her mother died, so she went to live with her grandparents. When her father married again a few years later, the second wife wasn't thrilled at the idea of a ready-made family, so my mother never came back here.'

Jaymie's eyes were wide with shock. 'Gretta never said a word about that.'

'Would you expect her to? It wasn't her fault, of course. She was only a child, and when she grew up she tried to re-establish contact. We came back a few times, but my mother was never really comfortable. And I don't think Gretta was entirely at ease either.'

'And you think leaving you the house was her way of trying to make it up to you?'

Simon looked around, his eyes filled with a coolness Jaymie had never seen there before. 'Either that or she was getting even by saddling me with all this.'

Jaymie didn't know how to answer that. No wonder he'd wanted to get rid of the house as soon as possible, she thought. And no wonder the list of material things he wished to keep was turning out to be such a short one.

The house was full of memories, she had said a few minutes ago. But this was the first time it had occurred to her that it was impossible for every single one of those memories to be a pleasant one.

They made a ridiculous-looking little procession as they crossed town to the Logans' ranch house. First there was Rob's multicolored vehicle, quieter and safer now that its new exhaust system was in place, but no more attractive than it had ever been. Then came Simon in a sporty red convertible—Jaymie had wondered if he'd driven it all the way from Atlanta, until she'd seen the Illinois plates. 'It's a rental,' he'd said, when he'd seen her looking it over. 'Too bad it's not a little warmer or I'd put the top down and take you for a ride.' Jaymie, dawdling a bit, brought up the rear in her little car.

The Logans' garage door was open and Van was inside filling a bird-feeder. 'Well, if it isn't a mobile parking lot,' he said drily. 'Haven't you all ever heard of carpooling?'

Rob feigned confusion. 'No. Is that a new Olympic event?'

'We're all going different directions after dinner, Dad.' Jaymie kissed her father's cheek. 'Rob, aren't you going to introduce your new pal?'

He gave her a cheeky grin. 'Of course not. You do that sort of thing so much better than I do, James.'

'That's why you need the practice.'

Van stretched out a hand to Simon. 'Don't mind them; they've been squabbling since before Rob could talk. I'm glad to meet you, Simon. Any friend of Jaymie's——'

'And Rob's,' she said under her breath. 'Don't forget Rob.'

'—is welcome in our home. Come in. Let Rob deal with your bags.'

In the kitchen, Carla was stirring the contents of a big sauce pot. She put her spoon down and offered her hand. 'We're so glad to have you come and stay with us, Simon. When Rob told me about the tower room— no heat, and full of boxes...'

Simon's smile was roughly a million watts of charisma—enough, Jaymie thought, to blow every fuse in town. She watched with reluctant appreciation as her mother succumbed to it. That was a relief, she thought. If Carla—whose years of teaching literature to high school students had made her a very good judge of character—had fallen so easily to Simon's charm, then it was no wonder Jaymie was starting to feel overwhelmed. After all, she was spending hours with him.

Simon was still holding Carla's hand, and smiling down at her. 'This is incredibly generous of you, Mrs Logan.'

'It's nothing,' Carla said. 'Jaymie started inviting friends home for meals when she was three, so I learned a long time ago to cook extra.'

Van said, 'Come along in and sit down, Simon. Jaymie's been keeping you busy over at the house, I understand?'

Jaymie didn't hear Simon's answer, just the slow music of his tone.

'What a beautiful voice he's got,' Carla said. 'Would you pull the rolls out of the oven, dear? I think they're done. I hope Simon likes fresh-baked bread.'

'Everybody likes fresh bread, Mother. And don't get any kooky ideas. You don't have to treat him like the King of Siam for my sake.'

'I beg your pardon, Jaymie? This is nothing special. Just spaghetti and homemade sauce.'

Jaymie rolled her eyes and considered putting her head in the oven and leaving it there. She settled for taking out the rolls, and helped carry the food into the dining-room. From Carla's attitude, she wasn't surprised to see the best china. But she was a little startled to see her grandmother's sterling-silver flatware laid out on the table as well, and fresh flowers in the centerpiece.

Right, Mom, she almost said. Just a simple meal. The kind of thing you do every night.

As soon as grace was over, Van poked his fork into the pile of spaghetti on his plate. 'Carla's trying to make you feel at home with Italian food, I see. Jaymie says you're in pizza.'

'I used to be, yes,' Simon said easily. 'At the moment I'm looking around for other opportunities.'

'Summerset's a good place for that,' Van said. 'Lots of activity here. Ever since the retirement community was built out at Paradise Valley and the Lassiter Trust invested in the mall, things have been hopping around here.'

Simon glanced at Jaymie, beside him. 'The mall where your shop is?'

She nodded. 'It used to be just a string of empty ware-houses, with Riley's restaurant the only lively spot for blocks.'

'And it's grown into *that*?'

'Well, don't let Dad make light of it—the project has taken several years and a whole lot of money.'

'And a mighty good investment it was, too,' Van pointed out. 'We're real proud of that one, down at the economic development office. We helped put the package together, you see.'

Jaymie wasn't listening. She broke a bite-sized chunk from her roll and mused, 'I wonder if the Lassiters would be interested in the house?'

'I thought they were still living in the studio apartment above the restaurant,' Van said.

'They are, but since the mall keeps expanding it's probably worth a fortune as retail space.'

'Then you're going to sell the house, Simon?' Carla asked.

'That's too bad.' Van shook his head sorrowfully. 'Summerset's doing very well, all things considered, but a town this size can always use some new blood. You might think about it, Simon. It's a good place to run a business, settle down, raise a family. Look at Jaymie, here——'

Jaymie closed her eyes in pain. Darn it, Daddy, she thought irritably. You don't have to point out that I'm available; it's already obvious!

'Don't mind Dad, Simon,' Rob said. 'He does this regularly.'

Aghast, Jaymie glared across the table at him. If Rob dared to suggest that Van made a practice of advertising her like this, she'd kick him. It wasn't true, and it was embarrassing enough without Rob getting into the act.

Though on the other hand, she realized, it might be better if Simon didn't feel he'd been especially singled out for this hard-sell approach. Was that what Rob was going to say? Maybe he wasn't such a bad brother after all...

Rob reached for another roll and said blandly, 'It's his job, you see. When you deal with local economic development, you have to be professionally optimistic about the whole town. Do you know how annoying it can be to listen to that all the time?'

Jaymie released the breath she'd been holding.

Rob eyed her with interest, and then winked and grinned. 'What did you think I was going to say, James?' he asked easily. 'Surely not something about you!'

CHAPTER SIX

SIMON put his fork down, wiped his lips, and reached for his wine glass. Jaymie sensed rather than saw the twitch in his fingers, and she thought in utter astonishment, The man's trembling as if he's terrified!

Then she realized it wasn't fear at all; Simon was doing his best not to laugh.

For one completely illogical instant, she was annoyed. Just what was so funny about the idea, anyway? She'd had plenty of steady boyfriends through the years and even a couple of marriage proposals. The only reason she wasn't dating much right now was sheer lack of time, not any shortage of opportunity.

So even though she might not be exactly to Simon's taste—she wondered for just a moment what sort of woman was—still, it wasn't completely ridiculous of her family to assume that he might find her attractive....

And why was she reacting so strongly, anyway? If it didn't matter——

But it did, she realized. What Simon thought of her was beginning to matter very much indeed.

The crazy breathlessness she'd felt this afternoon as she'd worked beside him came back in a rush. She told herself firmly that it was absolutely insane to feel this way, but it didn't help. She reminded herself that she scarcely knew the man, and that just last night he'd said he was living in deadly fear of her. That was no way to start a friendship, much less anything else—anything deeper. The whole thing was impossible.

And still she felt as if she was hyperventilating. She looked down at her plate and realized she'd eaten a good third of her spaghetti without having any idea what it tasted like. She hadn't been paying attention to anything but Simon—and no wonder, for just being around him was like parasailing off the edge of a cliff. It took all the attention one could muster just to maintain control.

But this was no time to think about the crazy way he affected her, that was certain. Jaymie realized that the table had been silent for what seemed forever; everyone but Simon was looking at her, and in another minute the whole scene would descend into farce.

Jaymie settled back in her chair and picked up her wine glass. 'What were you saying about Summerset, Dad?' Her voice wasn't shaky at all; she was proud of herself.

'Just that you're a symbol of the new breed of business person in town,' Van said.

Jaymie wanted to laugh at herself; she'd practically gone ballistic, and all her father had been talking about was Summerset Interiors. But somehow it wasn't as funny as it ought to be.

'And Rob can talk all he likes about my painful optimism, but it's no less true. Summerset *is* on the verge of a boom. This whole section of the country is going to be the next big development area, and we're poised to take advantage of it.' He turned to Simon with raised eyebrows. 'Do you want to get into a restaurant again, or do you have your eye on something different?'

'Something different, I think,' Simon said. 'I always did like new challenges. If you have any suggestions, sir...'

Rob shook his head. 'Now you've done it,' he muttered. 'I tried to warn you, Simon. By the way, you should never call him sir, either. It gives him a big head.'

'New challenges,' Jaymie mused. 'Does that mean you get bored easily?'

Simon turned to look at her, and smiled slowly. 'Only where jobs are concerned.'

The sparkle in the emerald depths of his eyes made Jaymie's mouth go dry with anticipation. She hadn't felt this way about a man since...she couldn't remember when. She'd never had quite this sensation before, that was sure.

And that was a scary thought. Why should she react so strongly to Simon, anyway? Was it just the lure of the unknown that drew her, the fascination that any stranger might hold?

And what was he feeling? Interest, certainly—she could see that in his eyes. But was it anything more than the thrill of pursuit he might feel with any woman?

'Well, there's the new industrial development out by the airport,' Van began. 'I expect you saw that as your plane came in. We've got plenty of sites and even some matching funds available for new industry—light manufacturing and that sort of thing. Of course it still takes some seed money, but——'

'Sounds like a great opportunity,' Simon said with an easy smile. 'It's too bad I don't know anything about manufacturing.'

'Then there's housing,' Van went on optimistically. 'Whoever gets in on the ground floor of housing construction in this town will make a fortune. Do you know anything about building houses?'

Simon shook his head sadly. 'Jaymie's teaching me to strip wallpaper, but I don't think that counts.'

Carla began to clear the table, and Jaymie got up to help her mother. A little later, when she brought in a big platter of fruit and cookies, she found the three men deep in a discussion about the college's basketball team and its chances for closing out the season on a winning streak.

'Not good,' she said, 'after their best shooter sprained his ankle last weekend.'

'They've got a game tonight,' Rob said, stabbing a chunk of Red Delicious apple. 'Want to go, Simon?'

'Yes, do go, Simon,' Carla said. 'If you like basketball, that is.'

Rob said practically, 'But if we don't want to miss the tip-off, we've got to leave now.' He munched a section of pear and picked up a big bunch of grapes and a handful of cookies as he pushed back his chair. 'Are you going, James?'

'Why? Do you want to borrow my season ticket?'

'Of course not. I've got my student pass,' Rob reminded her loftily. 'But Simon needs a ticket.'

Simon tilted his head to one side and looked up at her as she set a dessert plate in front of him. 'Why don't you come?' he asked softly. 'You said you like to cheer.'

'I should go back to the house and work.'

'How much did you expect to get done today?'

'One wall if I was lucky,' Jaymie admitted.

'And how much did we do?'

'Almost two. But——'

'Then you deserve a reward, don't you think?' His voice was even slower than usual, and it tugged at Jaymie's senses.

And, even more important, I want to go, Jaymie thought. Not so much to see the game, but to be with him. He might not stay for long...

'You certainly do deserve a reward,' Carla put in. 'Simon, Van will get you a house key right now, so you can come and go as you please. We want you to think of this as your home for as long as you like.'

'That's very sweet.' Simon picked up Carla's hand and brushed his lips softly against the back of it. Carla blushed like a teenager.

Jaymie's mouth dropped open. She was still speechless outside the house a couple of minutes later as Rob assessed the parking situation and said, 'We might as well take your car, James, since you left it in the way.'

She pulled herself together. 'Does that mean you don't have any gas?'

'How'd you guess? Unless you want to volunteer the convertible, Simon.' Rob flashed a grin. 'And since you don't know where we're going, I'll drive.'

'Nice try,' Simon said admiringly. 'You're not a bad kid, Rob, but I'm not turning my car over to you just yet.'

Rob, his pride uninjured, climbed into the back seat of Jaymie's car. 'That was smooth, Simon,' he said. 'Kissing Mom's hand, I mean. Maybe I should learn how to do that. It could have all kinds of uses.'

Jaymie gave a hoot of laughter.

Simon's eyes brightened, but he sounded serious. 'Oh, it does, and it's very easy, really. Subtlety is the key. Just a soft, quick brush of the lips...' He lifted Jaymie's hand off the gearshift and before she could pull away he'd kissed the back of each finger.

This is just a demonstration, she thought. He'd as good as said so, and therefore it was nothing which should be sending shivers running up her arm. But lecturing herself didn't stop the sensation, which was as delicious as ice-chips against sun-kissed skin on a hot summer day.

And Simon didn't let go. 'That's just beginner's level, of course,' he explained. 'The next step, Rob, is to flip her hand over and kiss her palm.' His voice was slightly muffled against Jaymie's skin as he demonstrated. 'And of course if you really want to cause a stir just dart your tongue against her lifeline like this——'

Jaymie pulled her hand away.

Simon leaned back in his seat. 'You seem a little flustered, Jaymie.'

'Of course I'm not, just ticklish.' There was a catch in her throat which made her sound a little huskier than usual. 'Besides, I need to turn here, and it's useful to have both hands.'

'I see.' The lazy note in his voice sounded like satisfaction.

'Flustered', she thought, was a mild word for what she was feeling!

The only empty parking spots were at the far end of the lot, and as they walked toward the basketball arena Rob hailed a group of his friends. 'I have to ask Jerry about a class,' he said. 'I'll be back.'

'Pity,' Simon murmured.

Jaymie took a deep breath of the chilly air. A little extra oxygen might help, she thought, but without any real confidence that it would make a difference. 'That Rob's coming back? I thought you were the one who said he was a great kid.'

'He is.' Simon reached for her hand and tucked it into the bend of his arm. 'I wasn't talking about Rob, anyway. I just meant it's a pity your hands suddenly became ticklish.'

Startled, Jaymie choked on nothing but cold air. 'What do you mean?'

'It didn't seem to be a problem when I was massaging them last night.' Simon smiled gently down at her and drew her a little closer to his side.

The auditorium was crowded. By the time Simon had bought his ticket, both teams were on the floor warming up, and the area where Jaymie usually sat was full. She led the way to a less crowded section, where Rob caught up with them. 'I'm going to get ice-cream before the game starts,' he announced. 'Anyone else?'

'Rob, how can you eat again so soon after all that spaghetti?'

'Because Millers' Malt Shop has a booth set up,' he said simply.

'Does that mean there's something special about this ice-cream?' Simon asked.

Jaymie nodded and sighed. 'It's Summerset's favorite food. Go on, I'll hold the seats. And don't bring me anything.'

They'd been gone only a couple of minutes when a platinum-blond perched on the seat next to Jaymie's. 'Hello, dear,' she cooed. 'The grapevine is whispering that you're going to be selling Gretta's house very soon.'

The grapevine, Jaymie thought, was nothing but gossip, and it was pure chance that in this case speculation had intersected with truth. Still, it was an illustration of Krista Blaine's business instincts; nothing went on in Summerset without her hearing about it. And since her business happened to be selling real estate . . .

'I don't know about *very* soon,' Jaymie parried. 'I can't actually give possession till after the showcase tours are over.'

'Then you'd better list it now.'

'What's happened to your self-confidence? I thought you could sell anything, in no time flat.'

Krista's smile bared her gleaming teeth. 'Relatively speaking, I can. To get the same results through another firm, you'd have had to list it months ago. Shall I get the papers ready and bring them over tomorrow?'

Jaymie considered. It was a big step; once she'd signed those papers there was no changing her mind. 'We'll have to talk about the details. There'll be some restrictions on showing it.'

'Of course. Tomorrow morning?'

Jaymie nodded. It had to be done, and for Simon's sake she might as well not postpone the listing. Still...
She glanced toward the floor where the teams were finishing their warmup and saw Simon and Rob headed toward her, each holding a double-dip ice-cream cone. 'Ten o'clock at my store,' she said briskly. 'We can talk about it all then.'

Krista was looking at Simon too, as if she too sensed the man's magnetic attraction. 'That's Gretta's nephew you're with tonight, isn't it?'

Jaymie nodded.

'Hmm. Well, I can understand why you're anxious to get rid of me.' She smiled sweetly. 'I'll see you tomorrow.'

Jaymie watched as Simon waded through the crowd toward her. He would have stood out in any crowd, she thought, and admitted that it was not the simple lure of the unknown which had attracted her, nor the interest she might have felt in just any stranger. What she felt for Simon was a much deeper fascination than that. He was a very special kind of man.

And if Jaymie wasn't careful she was apt to forget that the edge of danger about him could threaten her peace of mind for all time.

The home team won, though the game went down to the wire. Jaymie was practically hoarse by the time the basketball zipped through the net just as the final buzzer sounded.

'James really gets into basketball,' Rob told Simon. 'Of course, that might have something to do with the coach. She dated him for a while last winter. Is that why you're sitting all the way down here, James? So the coach won't see you with another man?'

Jaymie tried to suppress the embarrassed color which washed over her cheeks. 'Simon's not...' She stopped, a moment too late, as she saw the interest gleaming in Simon's eyes.

'Were you going to say I'm not just another man?' he speculated. 'Jaymie, what a flattering thing to tell me!'

She glared at him. 'I was starting to say, in a round-about way, that it's not the coach's business who I'm seeing. But since it's not yours either——'

'I am properly squashed,' Simon murmured. But his eyes were still sparkling, she noticed.

'And as for you, little brother...' Jaymie began.

Rob said hastily, 'I think I'll catch a ride with Jerry. Tell Mom I'll be home late because we're going out for pizza. Want to come, Simon?'

'No, thanks. I'll see your sister safely home.'

'Don't mind me,' Jaymie said. 'I don't need an escort. And why you'd be worried about me now when last night——'

'Besides,' Simon added smoothly, 'I'm so tired of pizza that I don't care if I never see it again.'

'That makes much more sense,' Jaymie muttered. 'Especially since we've got my car, and after I drop you off I'll be going home by myself anyway.'

'I'd forgotten. Then we'll go to your apartment instead, and I'll call a cab to take me back to your parents' house.'

'You could walk. It's only six blocks or so. But why? I'm not afraid to be out at night. The biggest crime in Summerset's history was a white-collar fraud a few years back.'

The parking lot was full of celebrating fans, and they could hardly go half a dozen steps before being stopped. If it wasn't a Service League member asking Jaymie about the showcase house, it was a resident welcoming Simon back to town.

'They all seem to assume I'm staying,' he mused.

'From their point of view, it makes sense. You've suddenly inherited the family property, so why wouldn't you want to stay? This is home, after all.'

'Not to me.'

'You haven't learned how people think around here. Once you belong to Summerset, you always belong.'

'But I've hardly even visited here.'

'Gretta was one of us, and that's close enough. A gap of a generation or two scarcely matters at all.' She smiled up at him. 'Don't fuss. When the house officially goes on the market, they'll be disappointed, of course. But it'll die down.'

'How long will that take?'

'Oh, I wouldn't worry about it. You'll be gone long before they stop talking about you.' Her tone was blithe, but underneath the empty feeling in the pit of her stomach reminded her that he wasn't likely to be around for long.

She turned toward the Logan house, and Simon objected. 'I don't have to be taken home.'

'I'm tired, Simon.'

'You'd be home earlier if you didn't take me all the way.'

She tossed him what she hoped was a mocking look. 'And you wouldn't want to come up for a drink, I suppose?'

'You don't trust me?' he said. He sounded almost plaintive, but she had no doubt that there was a mischievous glint in his eyes.

Jaymie didn't want to admit, even in her own mind, that it wasn't him she didn't trust, but herself. Considering the way she'd reacted last night when he'd kissed her, she had valid reason for doubt that she could invite him in for a drink and then send him on his way. Of course, she *had* been dead tired last night, and off her guard, so maybe...

Don't kid yourself, she ordered.

The Logan house was dark except for a dim light on the side porch, near the garage entrance. She pulled into the drive next to Simon's car, and let the engine idle.

'That brings back memories,' Jaymie said. 'Mother always left that light on when I was out on a date. I think she did it to remind me that lengthy goodnights were against the rules.'

Simon chuckled. 'It must feel very strange to be bringing me back here instead of going in yourself.'

'It does. It's weird, if you want the truth.'

'Well, if it will make you feel better...' His voice reminded her of honey on a warm afternoon, and Jaymie turned slowly toward him as if she'd been hypnotized. The lights on the car's control panel cast a soft glow over Simon's face, making his eyes look even bigger and darker.

She tipped her head back against his shoulder and admitted that she had been waiting for this moment. The anticipation had been building since this afternoon. Or maybe even since last night, when he'd kissed her and she'd wished he would never stop... Then his mouth brushed hers, and Jaymie stopped thinking.

The caress was as soft at first as when he had kissed her hand, but the tingles that had raced up her arm earlier in the evening were like mere static electricity compared to the lightning storm which jolted her now. His arms tightened about her and his kiss grew deeper and more intense, and Jaymie gave a little sigh and relaxed into his embrace.

The tip of Simon's index finger slowly traced an invisible line from the hollow at the base of her throat to her chin. 'Jaymie,' he whispered, 'we'd better cut this out or your mother will be shocked.'

She didn't want to let him go, but the hint of husky laughter in his voice brought her back to reluctant sanity.

He kissed her once more, very softly, got out of the car, and stood near the end of the drive, watching her until she was too far away to distinguish him from the shadows any longer.

Jaymie felt a bit shaky, as if she'd forgotten the finer points of how to drive a car. She was scared, that was the problem—and she didn't mind admitting it. Scared of Simon, and the effect he had on her. Scared of the intensity of her own reactions.

What did she know about him, anyway? Nothing, really, except that Gretta had adored him—which wasn't much of a recommendation, considering how seldom the woman had seen him.

Keep your distance, Jaymie told herself.

It was the only sensible thing to do—and she wished that she honestly thought she could manage to act on that shrewd advice.

Jaymie didn't see Simon for a couple of days, but it wasn't entirely on purpose, for several lots of furniture and draperies that she had ordered for her regular clients arrived ahead of schedule. It was exquisitely bad timing, Jaymie thought; even if she'd had room in the shop to store the things for a week or two, she couldn't bring herself to put off a customer. Installation and delivery took time, and she managed to stop at the Chadwick house only twice and stayed just long enough to check on the other decorators' progress.

Simon didn't happen to be there on either occasion. He'd spent some time in the house, though; it didn't take a genius to recognize his sense of humor in the way the books had been put back on the library shelves— lined up neatly by size and binding color without a hint of attention to each volume's subject.

Of course, the fact that she hadn't seen him didn't mean her confusion had gone away. If anything it was worse; she found herself thinking about him at the most inconvenient times and places, and she had a nasty suspicion that she'd cost herself business on a couple of occasions when her thoughts had wandered away from her clients at the wrong moment.

On Friday morning her assistant tracked her down—in a partially renovated office building where she was supervising a carpet-layer—to tell her that the painting contractor had a cancellation and would be at the Chadwick house at two that afternoon to paint the kitchen cabinets.

'But I can't be ready for him by then!' Jaymie wailed. Even as she was saying the words, however, she knew she would have to grab this opportunity. If she didn't, the contractor might put her off again, and there simply wasn't time for another delay. 'Connie, find Holly and plead with her to come and help me. We'll mask as fast as we can.'

An hour later Jaymie was standing on the stainless-steel counter near the refrigerator, taping newsprint to the tiled wall above the cabinets, when Holly arrived. 'Am I glad to see you,' Jaymie sighed. 'I was beginning to think you must have left town.'

'Wish I'd thought of it,' Holly mused. 'If that's all it takes to get me out of working... Actually, I figured you wouldn't want to stop for lunch, so I picked up some food at the malt shop. They've opened for the season already.'

Jaymie reached for another sheet of newsprint. 'Holly, you're terrific.'

'And tell me, what's Simon doing over there?'

Jaymie peered over a sheet of newsprint. 'Over where? At the malt shop, you mean? How should I know?'

'Don't try that tone of voice on me, my girl. The grapevine says the two of you are like this.' Holly held up a hand, fingers twined together.

'Well, grapevines are often wrong. I'd guess if Simon's hanging out at the malt shop it's because he adores the ice-cream—Rob introduced him to Summerset's favorite food at the basketball game this week. That's all I know about it.'

'I heard about that game.' Holly put the sandwiches and drinks in the refrigerator. 'I understand the assistant coach is going around with a hangdog look after seeing you with Simon, and——'

'Don't be ridiculous. I haven't even seen Simon since.'

'Oh? Now that leads to all sorts of interesting questions.'

'Would you shush and start taping, Holly?'

'I don't promise to stop thinking. Where do you want me to start?'

Jaymie paused and put her hands on her hips, heedless of the newspaper ink on her fingers. 'Mask the tiles between the upper and lower cabinets, and then start on the stainless steel. Leave the ceiling till last, because if we don't get it all covered——'

'You're kidding,' Holly gasped. 'You're planning to cover the whole ceiling?'

'If we have time. If not, I'll just have to let them paint and then scrape and patch up the areas where the overspray hits.'

For a few minutes, the only sounds in the kitchen were the rustle of paper, the rip of masking tape separating from the roll and the whisper of Jaymie's stocking-clad feet on the stainless steel. Then Holly said, 'It's too bad we don't have the budget to do this kitchen up right.'

'How would you do it?' To tell the truth, Jaymie was asking more to take her mind off the ache in her arms and the chill in her toes than because she truly longed for Holly's opinion. But if Holly was seriously interested in the house...

'Golden oak cabinets,' Holly said dreamily.

Jaymie looked at her in disbelief. 'You're joking. That doesn't fit into the original style of the house at all.'

'The Chadwicks put in bathrooms, didn't they? Those certainly weren't original.'

'That's a different thing altogether. The kitchen is perfectly nice just the way it is.'

Holly looked at her thoughtfully. 'Well, maybe when it doesn't look diseased any more, I'll see your point. Oops, there's only a few sheets of newspaper left.' She handed Jaymie the last section and vanished up the back stairs to look for more.

Jaymie wasted a precious couple of minutes wondering why the idea of golden oak cabinets bothered her so much. Holly was perfectly correct to say that updating a house wasn't a sin, particularly when it had been done before. The original kitchen probably hadn't had built-in cabinets at all.

It must just be that she was so happy with how the room was turning out that she couldn't stand to think of someone tearing it all out after all.

The back door banged and Simon came in. 'Well, hello,' he said cheerfully. 'The kitchen's certainly changed since I left.'

'Hi,' Jaymie said. She had to force herself to start taping again, because she would have much preferred to just stand there and look at Simon.

A moment later, she couldn't bear it any more, so she glanced at him over her shoulder. He was watching her, of course. Just my luck, she thought, to get caught sneaking a peek!

Since she was standing on the counter, Simon was at the precise angle of a fashion-show audience, looking up at a model on the runway. If she'd had any idea she'd end up in this position, Jaymie wouldn't have chosen the slimmest-cut pair of pants she owned. On the other hand, she decided, noting the way his eyes had narrowed, maybe she would have.

'Nice legs,' Simon said.

'Thank you.'

'I'd bet you took ballet lessons.'

'You'd win.' The words were brief, but the tone of voice added an edge of excitement to the exchange. Someone who was listening might think they were being curt, Jaymie thought. But there was a whole lot more going on underneath. 'Would you get me another roll of tape?'

Simon extracted one from the mess on the table and held it up. 'Want me to get each sheet ready and hand it to you?'

'Not at the moment, but stick around. When Holly finds more newspaper I'll put you to work.'

He reached into the refrigerator for a soda and sat down on the very corner of the kitchen table, swinging a foot and watching her work. 'Have you been avoiding me?' he asked.

Jaymie almost dropped the tape. 'Of course I haven't. I've been hanging draperies and delivering furniture.'

'Not around this house.'

She shook her head. 'That's true. Real-life clients can be so demanding,' she said, with mock-disapproval. 'Just because they're paying the bills, they think they have rights and should get service.'

'Imagine that,' Simon said agreeably. 'Silly fools. I can see why you'd much rather work for the Ideal Family.'

'You're right. Ideal people never complain.' She congratulated herself on successfully changing the subject.

'Of course,' Simon went on easily, 'I only asked if you were hiding out because your mother's wondering why you haven't been around, and because I keep running into men who look me over from head to toe as if I'm some kind of freak.'

'Who?'

'That's what I'd like to know. I can only assume that they're old boyfriends—or possibly current ones—who for some reason are feeling threatened.' He sounded as if he hadn't the vaguest idea why. 'You know, it would be thoughtful of you to warn me about the significant men in your life.'

The arrogance of the man made her want to scream.

'Of course Rob's filled me in on a few of the most recent ones, but——'

Before Jaymie could find her voice, Holly reappeared with an armful of newsprint.

'This is it,' she said cheerfully. 'The last stack in the house.' She eyed Simon and thrust a wad of paper at him. 'Oh, good. *You* can mask the ceiling, and if you don't get done in time Jaymie can put you to work straightening out the damage afterward.'

Simon set his soda aside. 'Where will I find a ladder?'

'On the back porch,' Jaymie said. She moved around the corner and started masking the area above the refrigerator. She'd like to slap a piece of paper over Simon's mouth. Asking for a rundown of the men she'd dated took a lot of nerve.

She wondered if he really wanted to know.

When Simon returned with the stepladder balanced on his shoulder, he was not alone. A woman in her mid-forties held the door for him and followed him in.

Lorilla Franklin, Jaymie thought in surprise. Now, what was she doing here? She wasn't even a member of the Service League, and she wasn't associated with any of the decorators either.

'If you're available for this sort of work,' Lorilla was saying to Simon, 'I'm always hearing of people who need a good handyman.'

'I'll keep it in mind,' he said easily.

'Sorry, Lorilla,' Holly said. 'Simon's just volunteering here in his spare time. He's too busy dipping ice-cream over at Millers' to take on another part-time job.'

He'd been *working* at Millers'? Was that what Holly had meant when she'd said she'd seen him there today?

Simon met her puzzled gaze and shrugged. 'They were busy with the lunch rush,' he said cheerfully, 'so I pitched in.'

'Helping out in a tight spot?' Jaymie asked.

'Yes, but I'll admit to some selfish motives, too. With enough practice, I'll be able to stack a mean triple-dipper cone, and you never know when that kind of experience will come in handy.'

Holly rolled her eyes. 'Well, Lorilla? What can we do for you today?'

The woman was at the dining-room door, reaching for the knob. She turned and gave Holly a humorless smile. 'Oh, don't mind me, I'm just looking around.'

'Not till the end of next week, you aren't,' Holly said firmly. 'And then you'll have to buy a ticket. The showcase isn't open for business yet.'

'I'm interested in buying the house. Krista Blaine sent me over.'

I doubt it, Jaymie thought. They'd made an agreement about the terms, and this visit violated them all. 'Krista and I agreed when I signed the listing that she'd call me before she planned to show the house, and she didn't. So I'm afraid you can't go through it today. Perhaps it would be better to wait till the work's done, anyway.'

Simon seemed to have frozen in position. He was holding a sheet of newsprint and looking at her—very oddly, Jaymie thought—over the edge of it. Obviously he didn't want to turn away a potential customer, but that was just too bad. Lorilla—and everyone else—would have to abide by the rules.

Lorilla clicked her tongue impatiently. 'That's exactly why I'm here—because the work isn't done. I want to turn the house into a restaurant and tea-room, you understand, and if I can just look at what you're doing I can save a lot of trouble. For instance, I don't know what you think you're doing with these cabinets, but there are city ordinances about what can be used in commercial kitchens. It would save a lot of waste if I just walk through and——'

'Straighten out our mistakes?' Jaymie said between clenched teeth. 'And perhaps you'd like to have approval of the wallpaper, too? I think you'd better talk to Krista again, Lorilla.' She reached down and took the sheet of newsprint out of Simon's hand, slapped it down on the top of the refrigerator and efficiently taped it into place.

Lorilla said, 'Well, if you aren't going to cooperate, I'll have to do just that. But I'll warn you, at this rate I may not be interested for long.' She slammed the door on her way out.

Simon was looking straight at Jaymie, but she sensed that he didn't really see her; he seemed to be staring into space. She bit her lip. 'Look, I'm sorry,' she began. 'But I'm sure Krista didn't send her. She might have mentioned the house, but she wouldn't encourage a self-guided tour. It's not good business. And I can't spare anyone to do the realtor's job this afternoon.'

'Oh, forget it,' Holly said. 'Lorilla's no great loss. How about a break for lunch before the malts have completely melted?' She reached for the handle of the refrigerator door. 'Jaymie, do you want the roast beef or the ham and cheese? Or shall we split them both? I assume you've already eaten, Simon?'

The door didn't open. Holly tugged again, as if she couldn't quite believe her senses, and then looked thoughtfully at the sheet of newspaper Jaymie had just put down atop the appliance.

'Honey,' she said, 'didn't it occur to you to wait till *after* lunch to tape the refrigerator shut?'

CHAPTER SEVEN

WHEN the painters arrived, Simon was draping the light fixtures with plastic, and Holly was arranging drop-cloths on the floor. Simon had pulled the huge old refrigerator out of its nook just far enough so that Jaymie could slip behind it to cover both the appliance and the wall with the last of the newspapers.

She had to smile at herself as she covered up the first layer of paper she'd so carelessly slapped on top of the refrigerator. It was taped on so tightly that Holly had had to rip the paper to get the door open and their food out.

That part had been funny, but the thought of Lorilla was enough to set Jaymie's teeth on edge. The woman had a lot of nerve to want approval of the decorating scheme before she even put an offer on the house.

The contractor came in, looked around, and grunted. 'Nothing to it,' he said, and summoned the rest of his crew with a gesture. 'We'll have this baby done in a few hours.'

Simon came down off the ladder. 'How soon should the paper be removed?'

'Oh, I'd give it a full day, so you won't take a chance on smearing the paint.' The contractor poked at his hat, pushing it back at a jaunty angle. 'If this stuff gets touched before it's completely dry, you'll never get the fingerprints out.'

'That's an idea,' Holly said. 'We could all line up to make our historic marks, like writing our names in concrete.'

Jaymie's hands were black from newspaper ink, and her skin was dry and itchy. She moved automatically to the sink to start washing up and then realized Holly had covered it with paper along with the counter-tops. 'If you need me,' she told the contractor, 'I'll be in the library—after I scrub my hands.'

Simon followed her down the hall. He was very close; much of the furniture from the downstairs rooms was still stacked in the hall, narrowing it to an inefficient passage, and Jaymie was achingly aware of the warmth of his body. Memories of that last kiss they'd shared— the way he had held her close, and the lightning which had seemed to flicker along her nerves—made her feel almost faint.

'I don't have any big plans for tomorrow,' he said. 'I'll take all the paper down in the kitchen when the paint's dry.'

'Would you?' Jaymie paused at the foot of the stairs. 'That would help a lot. I already have a list of things to do this weekend, and I don't dare go do them this afternoon, because if the painter has a question and I'm not around to answer it he might just take off.' She smiled up at him. 'Thanks, Simon. I'd never have gotten it done without you.'

'Remember that,' he said. 'I'm sometimes handy to have around.'

Jaymie could feel his warmth, and she knew that under the softness of his chamois-cloth shirt his shoulder would be solid and safe to rest against. At least, she'd be safe from the outside world, she reminded herself, but not particularly safe with him. Or with herself.

He leaned toward her, one hand braced on the tall newel post, and stared into her eyes for a few seconds that seemed to stretch into eternity. Jaymie's breath caught a little as she looked up into his eyes, and half consciously she wet her lips and waited for his kiss. How much she had missed him, in the last couple of days...

Then a door banged upstairs and one of the decorators started shouting, and the mesmerizing moment was broken. Jaymie tried to tell herself it was just as well, because the front hall was a bit too public for intimate caresses, but she couldn't quite erase the disappointment. There was an empty ache deep inside her.

Simon didn't move away, but he looked up the stairs toward the shouting. 'Sounds like someone's unhappy about the work,' he speculated.

'That's just Gloria. She's a dramatic type.'

'Is all this going to be done in time?'

Jaymie sighed. 'Of course it will.'

Simon smiled slowly. 'You don't sound convinced.'

'Oh, I admit I cut the schedule a little thin to start with, and then we got a slow start. But the House of Dreams will open on schedule, with a party, a week from tonight.'

'Then I shouldn't keep you from working, should I?' He tugged gently at a lock of her hair.

She tried not to let herself feel the tinge of regret. Even if the house was ahead of schedule, it wouldn't be safe to take the afternoon off and spend it with Simon.

'If you're looking for something to do——'

'I'm not.'

'Well, it is to your advantage to have it ready to show.'

'Oh, yes,' Simon said. 'I know. But now that you mention it, you didn't tell me you'd listed the house.'

'Didn't I?' She frowned. 'I was sure I had.' That reminded her of their unexpected visitor. 'Simon, you understand why I didn't let Lorilla wander around, don't you?'

'Oh, yes. But I'd have been happy to give her the tour. It might have been rather fun.'

The decorator came down the stairs. 'You won't believe what that idiot's done now,' she was storming. 'Jaymie——'

Simon slipped away while she was still soothing Gloria's feathers. Finally Jaymie managed to break free long enough to wash the newspaper ink off her hands. She slathered lotion on her abused skin and rubbed it in as she waited patiently to leave a message on Krista Blaine's answering machine.

Then she turned her attention to the library and started putting up the new blinds. She had chosen soft fabric panels which folded so tightly against the window-frame that they were almost invisible when fully open. But at night, she hoped, the blinds would close out the dark and the cold, creating a warm, cozy and cheerful room where any family would love to gather...

The Ideal Family. She could almost hear Gretta talking about them yet, laughing as she imagined the way they would work and live and love and play in her house, knowing it was only a game. Or had Gretta suspected—even as she'd entertained herself with the fantasy—that the time was closer than anyone wanted to think?

And now that the time was here, what sort of family would live in this house? Or would it be a family at all?

Jaymie forced herself to think about Lorilla's plans for the Chadwick mansion. The idea of the house being a business, not a home made Jaymie's heart ache, but she had to admit the sense of it. There were not a lot of families in Summerset with the financial resources to buy and restore and maintain a home of this size. It wasn't simply a matter of money, however, but of taste as well, for many of the people who could afford this house preferred the newer neighborhoods at the outskirts of the city.

And starting a tea-room wasn't a bad plan, either. Summerset was growing, but at the moment there was only one really good restaurant in town. A tea-room, close to downtown, with ample parking and the atmosphere of old family elegance, would fill a gap. It would attract bridge clubs, bridal showers, parties of all varieties—enough to build a good foundation for a business.

Jaymie couldn't quite see Lorilla, with her eccentric personality, being successful as a tea-room hostess, but that had nothing to do with the house. If the woman was wise enough to put someone else in charge of day-to-day operations, the business would probably succeed. And the house would pay for itself that way.

She blinked back a couple of tears and reminded herself that it was silly to assume that that was the way things would end up. Lorilla hadn't mentioned a price, so there was no way to tell yet whether the deal was feasible. She might not be willing to pay what the appraiser said the property was worth.

And there was Holly herself. She'd actually snapped at Lorilla. Had she simply been annoyed at the woman's presumption in wanting a decorating job done to her specifications, for free? Or had Holly been feeling a bit possessive about the house?

At any rate, until there was a valid offer on the table, it was incredibly silly for Jaymie to jump to conclusions. She'd just make sure the place looked its absolute best, and leave everything else to Krista. Once the tours began, surely someone would recognize what a wonderful house this was.

She hung the valances—simple rectangles of Paisley fabric draped artistically across hooks at the corners of the window-frames—and then dragged her ladder across to the bookshelves. Simon had lined the volumes up neatly, but Jaymie preferred a looser look, with blank spots here and there for collectables and photographs.

She still had to arrange the desktop—she'd found a very nice Victorian brass ink stand in the bottom drawer, and she'd bring over some of her own monogrammed stationery—and finish the shelves. But once those jobs were done and the newly covered furniture was returned, the library would be complete.

She wondered what Simon would think of the room when she was finished. He'd asked her a few days ago what sort of atmosphere she imagined for him, and she'd passed the question off with a light remark. She hadn't even known Simon when she had started to design the library, but, of all the rooms in the House of Dreams, this was the one she could most easily picture him in. Perhaps it was because this was where they'd spent their first hour together, but she could see him using this room, writing letters at the desk and piling books haphazardly on the shelves...

Holly popped her head in. 'Oh, there you are. Gloria wants to know where you put all the stuff from the dining-room cabinets. She needs the crystal goblets, and probably the china, too.'

Jaymie groaned. 'She's only now getting around to checking on it? The way she left all that glass sitting on the table, it's a wonder any of it survived!'

'I know. The woman's been more trouble...'

'It's up in the tower room, but I don't know which boxes. Simon might. Or Rob, if he's around.'

Holly vanished again, and Jaymie opened the bottom drawer of Gretta's desk and picked up a photograph. It was an old-fashioned sepia-toned shot of a bridal couple, the groom sitting straight in a brocade wing-backed chair, his bride standing rigidly beside him. Just the kind of thing the Ideal Couple would be sentimental about, she thought idly, and put it on the shelf. The groom was probably Simon's grandfather, she thought, noting the deep cleft in his chin. She wondered if it was his first or second marriage. Was the bride Simon's grandmother, or the second wife?

It was too bad she and Holly hadn't considered a wedding theme, she thought. What a brilliant idea that would be—an old-fashioned wedding, with the dining-room ready for a reception buffet, an arch in the parlor to shelter the ceremony, ribbons wound all the way down the banister with orange blossom and baby's breath twined around the spindles...

She smiled at herself. They had all they could handle as it was, but she was still coming up with new ideas. 'I should have my head examined,' she muttered.

'It's probably a little late for that,' Simon said. He came in and shut the door.

Jaymie's pulse speeded up a bit, but he didn't come directly to her. Instead he crossed the room and sank onto the window seat. His hair looked ruffled, as if he'd been walking in the wind.

'What have you been up to?'

'Wandering around the lawn. It's been a while since Gretta had anything done to the grounds, isn't it?'

'Well, it's a full block square, and she didn't have as much energy as when she was young.' Jaymie didn't stop arranging photos. She saw the level look he gave her, and expected that he would once more have something to say about the dilapidated condition of the house.

Instead, he said, 'I'm going down to the coffee-shop, since the kitchen is still off limits. Would you like to come?'

She hesitated, torn between desire and duty. 'Sorry, Simon. I really don't have time.' She turned back to the bottom drawer of the desk and picked up another framed photograph. 'I should probably poke my head in the kitchen in a minute to see how things are going.'

'I just did, and I don't recommend it.' He rose and picked up the frame she had just set on the shelf. 'Why are you using these?'

Jaymie hadn't paid any attention to the photo; she'd chosen it because the frame was a delicate gold filigree which contrasted nicely with the dark wood shelf. Now she realized it was a snapshot of Simon, one she didn't remember Gretta having on display. 'Because family photos give the proper ambience,' she said. 'What were you doing, anyway? White-water rafting?'

He nodded. 'Down the Snake River.'

Jaymie shivered. 'That's not my idea of a great vacation.'

'It was one of the least restful weeks I've ever had. That's what made it such a great trip.'

'If you say so.'

'What's your idea of a memorable vacation, Jaymie?'

Jaymie considered. 'Right now, I could go for lying on the deck of a cruise ship with a stack of good books and someone to bring me iced tea whenever I need a refill. Do you mind if I use some of the pictures, Simon?'

'Would it matter if I did?'

'Yes. I'd give them back to you and go dig up someone else's family photos.'

'Then I might as well save you the trouble.'

'Well, don't worry about losing them. I know they were on your list of things to keep, but they'll be safe in here, and I'll make sure they all get packed up for you afterward.'

He watched as she chose another couple of pictures. 'You seem to be lacking something,' he observed.

Jaymie surveyed the collection and turned to him with a question in her eyes. 'Like what?'

'There are no photographs which could possibly represent the Ideal Woman,' Simon pointed out.

'Oh—you're right. I hadn't noticed. Maybe she's the one who always has the camera.' She set another photo on the shelf. This one was of Simon with an older woman—his mother, perhaps, for she looked a bit like

Gretta—in what appeared to be a botanical garden full of azaleas. 'Have you always been in Atlanta?'

He shook his head. 'Just the last three years or so.'

'So that explains why your drawl isn't consistent.'

He smiled. 'It might. It's contagious, you know, but it takes a while to catch it.'

'So where were you before that?'

'Arizona for a while. Colorado. A few years in California.' He neatened the stack of books she'd pulled off the shelves to leave room for the pictures. 'Jaymie, I thought you were going to wait a while before you listed the house for sale.'

'I was. But then I realized I was worrying over nothing. Even if your hypothetical perfect buyer comes along——'

He looked puzzled.

'You know, someone who falls instantly in love with the house *and* has the cash in hand.'

'I remember talking about that, but——'

'Even then it would take several weeks to get through the formal appraisal and the title search and all the paperwork, and the tours would no doubt be finished by the time everything's done. So I decided it wasn't practical to put it off. It would only delay wrapping up the estate.'

Simon ran his fingers through his hair, messing it up even more. 'So you signed the listing.'

Jaymie nodded. 'I think you'll be happy with the results. Krista's the best in town, and very understanding of special needs. She'll be cautious about showing the house while the tours are going on, but at least if someone is interested we can be negotiating. It'll speed the whole thing up.'

'I see. Jaymie——'

Holly put her head in. 'Krista's on the phone.'

Jaymie moved toward the desk. 'Sorry, Simon. I asked her to call me.'

He waved a hand and retreated to the window seat.

'Hi,' Krista said. 'You must have been reading my mind when you left that message about needing to talk to me. I've got a signed offer. When can I bring it over for you to look at?'

'Already?' Jaymie said faintly. At the least, the document was a starting point for negotiations; at the most—if the price was right and the rest of the terms acceptable—it needed only Jaymie's signature to be a legal contract. And, no matter what she'd just told Simon, she wasn't ready for this.

Then she took a deep breath and pulled herself together. What had happened was obvious, and there was no need to panic.

'I thought Lorilla was being a little hasty when she said she wasn't interested any more,' Jaymie said, 'but I didn't expect she'd go this far the other direction.'

'Lorilla? What are you talking about?'

'Isn't the offer from her? She said you'd told her about the house.'

'I mentioned it, yes. It was a slip of the tongue, actually. But how do you know about that?'

Jaymie told her about Lorilla's aborted tour.

Krista groaned. 'I'm sorry. I put off arranging a showing for her because frankly I don't think she can afford to buy it. I certainly didn't send her over to tour the place on her own.'

'I didn't think you would. But if this offer isn't from Lorilla, who is it from?'

'I really can't go into it on the phone, Jaymie. It's the rule that an offer has to be presented in person. I've got an appointment right now, but can I pop over and talk to you in a couple of hours?'

Jaymie agreed and put the phone down. 'Well, that was prompt,' she said, and tried to laugh. 'Now that I come face to face with your hypothetical buyer, I have to admit I didn't believe it was possible anyone would jump at this place that fast.'

Simon didn't sound amused. 'Jaymie, this is the last thing you need this afternoon. You're exhausted, you're busy——'

'True. But what do you suggest I do about it?'

'Turn this over to me. Let me take care of Krista and the offer.'

She was astounded. 'But I can't. I'm the executor, so I can't just give up all responsibility.'

'Of course not,' Simon said softly. 'But I can weed out the obvious.'

'You mean, if the price is too low——'

'Exactly. Why take up your time right now with something that isn't even reasonable?'

It made sense. And it wasn't that she didn't trust Simon's judgment; after all, it was his money which was involved. And he couldn't agree to any kind of deal without getting her approval as well. 'If there's any doubt, you'll ask me?'

He just looked at her, one eyebrow quirked.

Stupid question, Jaymie told herself. Of course he would. 'All right,' she said finally. 'I can use all the help I can get. Krista said she'd be over in a couple of hours.'

'Then I'll go get my coffee now. Would you like me to bring you something?'

Jaymie shook her head.

Simon stopped at the door. 'By the way, you mentioned the opening-night party. What's going on?'

'It's nothing all that elaborate, really, just an excuse to sell very expensive tickets. You'll be there, won't you? Since you're sort of the official host, since Gretta can't be there...' She bit her lip at the thought of how much

Gretta would have enjoyed that party, and tried to smile. 'We won't make you pay, of course.'

'Oh, that's a relief.'

The deadpan humor helped her put her sorrow aside. 'Well, you'd only be getting half the value anyway. We sold the tickets early, and they included two parties—a brunch we held a couple of weeks before Gretta got sick, so people could see the house before we started work, and then desserts and coffee and liqueurs on opening night.'

'I see.'

Jaymie looked at him curiously. 'You sound disappointed.'

Simon shrugged. 'A late-evening party messes up my plans. I thought if it was just cocktails I'd treat your parents to dinner afterwards as thanks for taking me in. At least, I assume you didn't miss the chance to sell them tickets?'

'As a matter of fact, the tickets were a gift for their wedding anniversary, but you're right about them coming to the party. Maybe you can take them out to dinner another night.'

'I wasn't planning on going out, exactly. I thought it might be fun to have dinner here.'

'Gloria would probably have an attack if you actually used her table setting,' Jaymie said absently.

'Why should she? It's technically my house. For the moment, at least.'

When he'd gone, Jaymie put the last group of pictures into place and stood back to look over the shelves with a bit of pride. It had that certain careless touch she'd been aiming for—not at all like a purposeful display. Many of the books stood at angles, as if they'd been well-read, then gathered up and pushed back onto the shelf in a bunch. And the pictures seemed to have been added to over the years, as the family grew and changed.

The Ideal Family... too bad she didn't have any snapshots of babies and small children to include. Maybe Holly would bring in some pictures of her kids. Jaymie could probably find something to represent the Ideal Woman in her own photo albums; heaven knew she had thousands of snapshots of her friends. Though she had to admit she liked the explanation she'd given Simon even better; maybe she'd just let the Ideal Woman remain a mystery. That way every female who toured the house could put herself in the Ideal Woman's shoes, and pretend that Simon was her ideal man...

That wouldn't be hard to do, she thought. Oh, no—it wasn't hard at all. She didn't even have to close her eyes to picture him in this room and in this house. And as for picturing Simon as a very large and important part of her life...

Wasn't it about time she stopped playing games, Jaymie asked herself, and admitted that she could fall in love with Simon Nichols without any effort at all?

Except that perhaps even that wasn't going far enough. Perhaps she already loved him.

Simon had been right; when Jaymie cautiously peeked around the edge of the kitchen door, she almost choked on the smell of paint. But the work was done and the men were packing up their equipment. They looked a bit like gigantic insects in their respirators and coveralls.

The cabinets had a new glow which more than justified the time and money she'd spent in restoring them to life. She couldn't wait to see what the room would look like once the papers were down. Would the blue-gray sheen add warmth and comfort to the room, balancing the coldness of the tiles and stainless steel as she had hoped it would? How she wished Gretta could see this...

The contractor handed her a clipboard, and she signed the work order. 'Better put a mask on,' he said gruffly. 'Or else get out of here—there's no reason to be breathing these fumes.'

'I just wanted to get a glimpse. You said to wait twenty-four hours before we take the papers down, right?'

'That would be safest. You might want to unwrap the refrigerator right away, though. Those old appliances generate a lot of heat, and you wouldn't want the compressor to set the paper on fire and burn the whole house down.'

Jaymie took the filtration mask he handed her, and as soon as the men left she started to peel newspaper off the back of the refrigerator. It was a slow job; though the paint on the papers seemed dry, it rubbed off on her fingers, and keeping it away from her clothes was a first-class challenge.

'I should have left this for Simon to do,' she muttered. 'If he was thoughtful enough to volunteer, I should have let him.'

Finally she resorted to tearing off the paper one small panel at a time and folding each piece neatly into a garbage bag before going back for another. But eventually the cooling coils were uncovered, and the door opened freely again. She dragged a chair over and started on the top of the appliance.

She wasn't sure why the headline caught her eye. She seldom paid much heed to the business sections of the Chicago newspapers, and in the last few weeks she certainly hadn't had time to read them. In this case, perhaps it was the word pizza which grabbed her attention, combined with the fact that lunch seemed entirely too long ago. She was beginning to regret telling Simon that she didn't want anything from the coffee-shop. They had the best pizza in Summerset, and a hot slice of pepperoni with black olives would really hit the spot just about now...

'Pizza king sells empire', the headline said. She read the first paragraph just to torment herself with the thought of hot cheese and spicy tomato sauce and crisp, chewy crust.

Then she put both elbows down on the paper, heedless of the specks of paint which soaked through her sleeves, and read the rest of the story—all about Simon Nichols, the hundred pizza parlors that he'd built from a single mall restaurant, and the fortune he'd collected just last month when he'd sold the entire chain.

CHAPTER EIGHT

SIMON was unemployed, all right, Jaymie reflected. But only because he'd chosen to be. He hadn't been fired or even laid off.

He'd told her the business had been bought out and the new owners no longer needed him. That, apparently, was the absolute literal truth, but the way he'd said it had turned the simple fact into...not a lie, perhaps; that would be putting it a little strongly. But it hadn't been an accidental misstatement either. He'd phrased it that way on purpose, to be misleading.

And that wasn't the only example. When Van Logan had asked about the pizza business, Simon had sidestepped the question. Only now, when Jaymie thought about it, did she realize how very little he'd really said.

He'd also been careful when talking about money. He hadn't said he couldn't afford a hotel; he'd just announced his intention to stay at the Chadwick house, and Jaymie had drawn her own conclusions about his finances. Fool that she was, she'd felt so sympathetic for him and so anxious to get the estate settled for his sake that she'd ignored the evidence of her own eyes—the little red convertible, the expensive clothes, the fact that he never seemed to be short of cash.

He'd had a multitude of chances to make everything clear—but he hadn't. He hadn't precisely told lies, she admitted that. But that fact didn't win him any points as far as Jaymie was concerned, for he had deliberately misled her, and from her point of view it ended up being exactly the same thing.

No wonder he'd stood like a statue in the kitchen this afternoon staring at a sheet of newspaper—this very sheet of newspaper. Jaymie had thought at the time that he was upset because she'd refused to let Lorilla Franklin tour the house. But that hadn't been it at all; he'd just spotted this story, which he obviously hadn't expected to see. He must have been debating how to get it out of sight.

That explained why he'd looked so startled when Jaymie had taken the paper out of his hands and taped it to the top of the refrigerator. And it also accounted for his volunteering so generously to come in as soon as the paint was dry and strip the papers himself. She hadn't even questioned the offer at the time; it had seemed so like Simon to volunteer. But now she wondered just how far he'd have gone to keep his secret.

She had honestly believed that the initial suspicions each of them had felt on the day Gretta's will was read had been left behind as they'd started to build a friendship. So much for that idea! What lay between them wasn't anything resembling friendship after all. It had been nothing more than a facade on Simon's part, and it was no comfort at all to remember that from the very beginning she'd had her doubts about this enticing stranger.

Anger flared deep inside her. She felt used, almost violated. She'd considered him to be a friend; she'd never given Simon a reason to doubt her own honesty. And this was how he paid her back! Well, friends didn't treat each other like this—with lies and concealment and handy half-truths.

And as for the idea that he could ever be more than a friend—well, she was truly a fool if she believed she could love a man who hid himself so thoroughly, a man who treated her as Simon had.

*   *   *

Jaymie was still there when Krista came to the back door. The painters had slit the papers over the door so that they could leave, but it was still covered, and Krista peeked in and made a face. 'What are you doing in here? Auto-body repair? Heavens, what a smell!' She closed the door behind her. 'I hope you don't mind if I'm a little early.'

Jaymie tore another strip of newspaper off the refrigerator. 'It doesn't matter to me, because Simon's going to——' She stopped abruptly. Simon was going to consider the offer, she'd almost said. He'd offered to help her out; at least, that was how he'd phrased it. But could she trust him on that, either?

'Simon's going to what?' Krista asked inelegantly.

'Never mind.' Jaymie pushed the strip of paper into the garbage bag and held out a hand. 'I'll look at it.'

'In here? Do you know you've got paint all over you, Jaymie?' Krista sighed and handed over an envelope. 'I'll say one thing for the surroundings you've chosen,' she mused. 'I'll certainly try my best to keep the proceedings brief.'

'There's an extra mask somewhere.' Jaymie unfolded a single, closely typed legal form. 'Who could be putting an offer on this place, anyway? Nobody's even been through it, except Service League members. Is it one of them?'

'No. It's someone who's wanted it for a long time. And before you even look at the bottom line, Jaymie, remember that I'm bound by law to give you any offer, no matter how low the price or how ridiculous the conditions. You don't have to accept it, of course, but I have to show it to you.'

Jaymie recognized the name on the contract. The man owned Knox Associates, the best-known construction company in Summerset County. 'I'd have expected him to build himself a new house, not buy an old one,' she said, and glanced at the offered price. It was scarcely a third of what they'd decided to ask. 'I see the low price. What did you mean about the ridiculous conditions?'

Krista shifted from one foot to the other. 'I was speaking loosely.'

Jaymie refolded the contract and looked at Krista with suspicion in her eyes. 'Are you still working for me, or have you switched sides?'

'Of course I'm still working for you. A realtor always...' She sighed. 'I wasn't going to tell you. I thought there was no point in upsetting you, because you're going to turn the offer down anyway, right? But you're not going to quit till you know, are you, Jaymie?'

Jaymie shook her head. 'Especially not after you've said that much.'

'He's not particularly interested in the house.'

Jaymie frowned. 'Then why is he offering to buy it?'

'He plans to tear it down for salvage and use the lots to build apartments.'

Jaymie thought for a moment that the floor was sliding out from under her feet. '*Tear the house down*? Krista, I can't allow anything like that!'

'I know,' Krista said hastily. 'Just remember it wasn't my idea. I didn't even call the guy, Jaymie. He figured you'd be selling sooner or later and he wanted to get the first bid in, so he came to me. He didn't even know you'd listed it yet.'

'This is the most preposterous, bizarre, incredible——'

Krista said, 'Don't get crazy on me, Jaymie. I couldn't refuse to bring you the offer, but all you have to say is no and that's the end of it, unless he wants to increase the price.'

The dining-room door creaked open. 'I looked all over for you,' Simon said. 'I should have guessed I'd find you in here admiring the results. You just couldn't wait to see it, could you?'

Jaymie wheeled around to face him; he was leaning against the door jamb with a foam coffee-cup in one hand. What a perfect fraud the man was, she thought furiously. He actually sounded calm—as if there wasn't a thing on his mind.

Fury boiled up inside her, and her self-control snapped. She pulled the refrigerator door open, grabbed the first thing she saw—which happened to be an orange left over from someone's brown-bag lunch—and threw it at him as hard as she could. She hoped the orange was a juicy one; it would be satisfying to watch pulp spray all over him.

Simon side-stepped and put out a hand, and the orange slammed into his palm with a smack. 'Not a bad pitch,' he said. 'You could teach the Ideal Child something about softball.'

Jaymie reached into the refrigerator again. If she was lucky, there'd be something a whole lot harder than an orange.

'Just a minute,' Simon said. He took a couple of cautious steps forward and set the orange on the kitchen table. 'I'd guess that under the mask you're not smiling.'

'Give the man a prize,' Jaymie muttered.

Krista, who had been looking back and forth between them in puzzlement, held out her business card. 'I'm Krista Blaine,' she murmured. 'Friendly neighborhood real estate person.'

Simon shifted his coffee-cup and shook her hand. 'I've been wanting to meet you. Now I remember—you were talking to Jaymie at the basketball game.'

Krista smiled. 'I had no idea you'd noticed.'

Jaymie rolled her eyes in disbelief.

'Is that why Jaymie's throwing things at me?' Simon went on. 'Because I wasn't here on time to look at an offer? I'm sorry. Let's go into——'

'You don't need to look at anything,' Jaymie said. 'I've already decided.'

He took a long swallow of coffee and looked at her steadily. 'And the verdict is?'

'I'm not accepting the offer.' She turned to Krista. 'And even if the man meets the price we set, I'm still not going to take his offer. So you might as well tell him that right now and save us all a lot of paperwork.'

Simon's eyebrows went up. He pushed the drop-cloth off the table and sat down on the corner of it. 'Might I be allowed to inquire why you've suddenly lost interest in selling?' he asked mildly.

'It isn't that, it's the conditions.' She thrust the contract at him. 'I wouldn't consider selling to him at any price. Simon, he wants to tear the house down and build apartments!'

'Well, it would be his to do with whatever he liked.'

Jaymie glared at him. Even if he didn't have any sentimental attachment to the house, surely he had some artistic appreciation of its beauty, some desire to see it preserved . . .

On the other hand, maybe he didn't.

'I suppose you're delighted that somebody thinks we're sitting on a valuable block of land,' she snapped.

Simon studied her thoughtfully for a moment. 'It's not a bad idea, you know,' he said finally. 'I can see his point. This whole square block, close to downtown, the college, and the mall . . . If what your dad said about the housing shortage in Summerset was true, this could be a nice little development.'

'Don't you even care what happens to it?'

'I'm just being practical. Once it's sold, that's not my business. Or yours. You can't put restrictions on what the next owner does, you know.'

'Well, I don't have to sell it to this guy!'

'True. But even if you insist on a promise not to tear the house down, it won't be any guarantee the place will survive in the long run. You'll have only the buyer's word to go on, and once the paperwork's done you don't have anything further to say about it. The new owner could swear to preserve it and still send the bulldozers in, or sell it again to someone else who will.'

Tears stung her eyes. He was very logical, and very correct. But Simon didn't see things in the same way that Jaymie did. The town wasn't a part of him as it was of her; the house hadn't taken root in his heart. He wouldn't be here to see the results, to note the gap in what passed for Summerset's skyline. He didn't care—and that made her furious.

But she hadn't been asked to preserve the house. Her job as Gretta's executor was to make certain that the estate produced the maximum value for the heir, and the fact that it would break her heart to see this grand old mansion battered into dust didn't matter at all.

'So I might just as well accept the best offer,' she said tartly, 'and close my eyes to the results, as long as it means you get the most money possible out of the deal. All right, that's what I'll do. But this particular offer's still dead—it's not nearly enough cash.' She took the contract out of Simon's hand, ripped it decisively into quarters, and thrust the pieces at Krista. 'If your customer's got a better offer, I'll look at it. And if he wants to pay the price, then I'll stand right here and watch the bulldozers.'

Krista looked at the wad of paper in her hand and sighed. 'I'll tell him,' she said. 'And I imagine I'll be back in touch in a day or two.'

The back door closed behind her, and silence settled over the kitchen. Jaymie ripped a strip of paper off the tile wall beside the refrigerator; the sound seemed to echo. Simon shifted his weight, and the table creaked.

Why didn't he just go away? she wondered.

'Do you mind telling me what's really going on?' he said finally.

'Tearing down the house isn't enough?'

'Jaymie, for heaven's sake...' He sighed. 'Why have you been pulling down the papers anyway? The painters said not to do it for a couple of days, and I told you I'd take care of it, when it's time.'

'And I know why you volunteered so readily, too. You saw that article, didn't you? The one about the pizza king of Georgia.'

His eyes narrowed, but there was no other visible reaction, and for a moment she thought he was going to deny it. 'Yes, I saw it.' He sounded almost wary.

'A hundred pizza parlors,' she mused. 'So much for that cute little tale about being allowed to run the cash register once in a while—between mopping floors and clearing tables, if I remember it correctly.'

'I did all that,' he said. 'At least half a day a week I'd visit one of the restaurants, do a regular job, talk to the customers about the food and the service. That's how I got into pizza in the first place—the restaurant produced a great-tasting meal, but the service was lousy. So I bought it. Once it started to straighten out, another one came along, and another...'

'And before you knew it there were a hundred.'

'Something like that.'

'What a wonderful down-home story. I'd have thought you'd be proud of it, not trying to hide it.' She held the paint-stained newspaper up to study the headline once more.

'You expect me to walk around with a stack of re-prints, passing them out? So what if I was going to let that article disappear? I have my reasons.'

'Oh, I can't wait to hear them.'

'I'll bet.' His voice was crisp and cool. 'But if you can't figure them out on your own, I don't see any advantage in explaining.'

Jaymie bit back a sharp accusation. Yelling at him wouldn't get her anywhere; Simon obviously didn't think he owed her any answers. It was only her own fool-ishness which said there had been a growing closeness between them, a developing friendship—or more—which had been violated by his lack of trust. She said acidly, 'Too bad for you that the painters weren't just a bit sloppier.'

'It might have saved a little trouble,' Simon agreed. 'Dammit, Jaymie——'

'Oh, you don't have to explain anything to me. I'm tickled to death at being singled out to look like a fool. If you want to be a mystery man, Simon, why are you hanging around Summerset? Or maybe you've for-gotten that nobody asked you to come here, and no-body's asking you to stay.'

'Don't you think it would look a little odd if I left now?'

'Who cares?' She turned her back on him and began to scrape at a strip of tape with her fingernail. 'If anyone asks, just tell him you're going back into the pizza business.'

'I can't,' he said mildly. 'I signed a non-competition clause when I sold out. Not that it matters—now that I've done pizza once, I can't imagine doing it again.'

'Oh, yes, I remember you saying something about being easily bored by your work.'

'I said I liked challenges.'

'Oh, was that it? I'm sure there are great opportunities somewhere in the world right now for the pizza king of Georgia.'

'Somewhere besides Summerset, you mean?'

'Now you're getting it,' Jaymie said, with a note of congratulation in her voice. 'I don't care what you do, Simon. I'm just going to finish my job the best way I know how—both the showcase and the estate. So why don't you go away so I can work in peace?'

He didn't even answer, and he moved so quietly that she didn't hear him leave. A moment later, however, when she sneaked a look, he was gone.

Jaymie finished unmasking the refrigerator, but the smell of paint was too strong to let her go any further. At least the fumes made a handy explanation for why her eyes were stinging and her head ached.

Jaymie didn't see Simon over the weekend. Had he left Summerset altogether, or was she missing him by sheer chance? Of course, she had to admit that she was staying as far away from the house herself as she could, and if he was doing the same...

By Monday, the pressure was building. She had three rooms and a bath to finish, and she couldn't work by remote control; she would have to spend most of the week at the Chadwick house. But she couldn't concentrate if she was wondering all the time whether Simon was likely to pop up. And he seemed to be the only thing she could think of. When she looked at a paint chip, she remembered him telling her to send him samples. When she looked at the striped wallpaper waiting to be hung in the guest room, she thought of the afternoon they'd talked about her vision for that room. And just going into the library brought pain, for she had to admit that the finishing touches there had all been done with

Simon's pleasure in mind. She had brushed aside the Ideal Man and decorated that room for Simon.

Finally she swallowed her pride and asked Rob, who was shifting Jaymie's rose velvet parlor suite back into the finished front room.

He looked at her as if she'd suddenly turned into a pumpkin and said, 'Simon went to St Louis yesterday.'

'Did he stay there or go on somewhere from the airport?'

'How should I know?'

'Did he say if he was coming back?'

Rob frowned. 'Now that you mention it, no. I just assumed . . . Sorry, James. If I'd known it was important I'd have asked.'

'Who said it was important?' Jaymie said. She managed just the right tart tone, but she had to bite her lip to keep tears from forming.

Rob stared at her in shock, then awkwardly put an arm around her and patted her back. 'I'll find out, James.'

She put her head down on his shoulder, but she couldn't quite give in. 'It really doesn't matter. I'm just so tired, Rob. That's all.'

'Right,' he said soothingly. 'Of course I believe you. And don't worry, I won't tell Mom or Dad that you're the one who wants to know where Simon is.'

She had to laugh at that. 'Oh, Robbie, you're the best of brothers!'

He grinned at her. 'Does this mean you'll forgive the rest of my car repair bill?'

She wiped her eyes and went up to the guest room feeling a little better. At least she could get down to work with a clear mind. She was dressed in her oldest sweat suit, and she intended to stay around the clock, if necessary—as long as it took to strip the rest of the old paper and prepare the walls for the plaster repairman and the paper-hangers.

She was really pushing time, for it would take a full day to patch the damaged sections and most of another to hang the new wallpaper. And there was still the kitchen to finish—but she could be doing that while the paper-hangers were working.

Though she didn't find it a great deal of comfort, Jaymie wasn't the only one who was running right down to the wire. The master bedroom had been completed over the weekend, but the nursery was still in progress, and as Jaymie climbed the stairs she could hear the high-pitched whine of an electric saw from the bedroom Gretta had designated for the Ideal Child. The sound grated on her nerves.

Jaymie closed her eyes as she turned the knob of the guest-room door and told herself that if she looked at only one wall, one section at a time the remaining task would seem more manageable.

But instead of the chipped and ragged paper she expected to see still clinging in random patterns as it had been on Friday—the last time she'd checked the room—she saw bare plaster. The walls were still streaked with paste, but the heavy work was done.

She stood in the center of the room and turned in a slow circle, unable to believe what she was seeing. It had never occurred to her that Simon would come up here and finish the work over the weekend. After the quarrel they'd had, she would have expected him to stay as far away as possible.

Why had he done it? An honest wish to help? Or a tinge of guilt, perhaps; his offer to finish the kitchen work hadn't exactly been for the purest of reasons, and maybe he was trying to make up for it. Or was this a roundabout way of saying he was sorry for the way he'd treated her, for the fight they'd had and the distance between them?

Don't even dream of something like that, she told herself. It would hurt too much if it turned out not to be true. He might just as easily have finished because of sheer determination not to quit. Simon was like that—whatever he decided to tackle, he would do.

Jaymie leaned against the wide marble ledge at the base of a window and tried to fight off tears. She told herself firmly that it was silly to picture him as the Ideal Man. He was far from that. The Ideal Man was a solid kind of guy, handsome, good-natured... After the quarrel they'd had, no one could call Simon good-natured!

No, he wasn't the Ideal Man Gretta had described, who was dependable and hard-working—'And so perfect that he'd be pretty dull and boring in real life,' she muttered. Simon was far from dull—he was impulsive and unpredictable. And as for being reliable...

Well, much as she'd like at the moment to deny that he had any virtues at all, she couldn't deny that a man didn't make a success of a string of a hundred pizza parlors without a good deal of effort. And he was also funny, generous, handsome...

No, he wasn't the Ideal Man Gretta had described, but in many ways he was a whole lot better.

And, ideal or not, he was the man she loved. The man she would always love, whether she ever saw him again or not.

Late the next afternoon Jaymie was hanging new curtains in the kitchen, and wondering, despite her best efforts, what Simon would have thought of them, when Gretta's attorney knocked at the back door. She had to climb down from a chair to let him in. 'Sorry the door was locked, Herbert,' she said. 'The closer we get to opening, the more people seem to have an excuse to drop by. One of them got all the way to the tower yesterday before we caught her, and then she said rather feebly that she was looking for a friend who'd told her she might be here.'

Herbert chuckled. 'That kind of interest holds promise for the tours, I'd say.'

'Oh, the advance tickets are selling very well.' She poured a cup of coffee from the pot she'd just made and handed it to him. 'Everyone wants to see the House of Dreams.'

Herbert looked around and then sat down at the table. 'Well, I don't think people will be disappointed. The place looks a whole lot different.'

Jaymie followed his gaze. She'd been right about the color of the cabinets; the room felt much warmer now, and the addition of the curtains—soft, puffy panels in a floral print which picked up the dusty blue-gray of the cabinets and mixed it with a host of brighter colors—softened the atmosphere even more. 'It feels disloyal, in a way, to change it so much, even though Gretta approved every bit of the work. And I know she would have loved the results. Still...'

And it feels even more disloyal, she thought, to know that in a few months all this might well be gone. Everything Gretta cared about could be crumbled into dust and replaced with a row of apartment houses.

Time to stop that nonsense, Jaymie told herself. She'd take the best offer, whatever it was, and that would be the end of her involvement. 'Anyway, Herbert, thanks for stopping over. I'd have been happy to come to the office...'

Herbert shrugged. 'No inconvenience at all. It's on my way, and I have some things to talk to you about, too.'

'Like what?'

'Oh, we'll get to that. It's nice to see the place looking like a real home again. It needs a young family, a growing one.'

Jaymie looked down at her cup. A young family, she thought. A growing one. The kind of family she wanted to have someday, with so much love to give that, no matter how big the house they lived in, it would overflow... The kind of family she could have created with Simon, if only he had cared as much about her as she did about him.

But it was foolish to think of things like that. If she'd been at all important to him, he wouldn't have hidden all the vital facts that he had kept to himself, would he?

'Well, there don't seem to be any young families in the market for a house just now.' She cleared her throat. 'The reason I called you, Herbert, was to ask if I can buy things from the estate.'

Herbert tipped his head to one side. For a moment he looked very much like a robin—bright-eyed and inquisitive. 'Like what sort of things?'

'There's some china and crystal and a few pieces of furniture I'd like to have. But since I'm the executor I didn't know if I could make myself a deal.'

'Yes, you can. The best way is to have an independent appraiser look at everything, so no one can question whether you're cheating the estate.'

'By "no one" you mean Simon, of course?' Jaymie said flatly.

Herbert shook his head. 'Oh, I doubt Simon would be concerned. But other observers, and the court, might wonder if you were being fair, and then there's always the tax problem...'

'In that case, I'll skip it. An appraisal would be expensive, and I doubt the things I want are worth more than a few dollars.'

'The simplest thing would be to wait till the auction. If you buy something then, there can't be any question about a fair price or a conflict of interest. Have you set a date?'

Jaymie nodded. 'The first weekend in May, right after the tours are over. It won't give me a lot of time to get ready, but the auction company promised to send lots of help to fetch and carry and sort and unpack, so I guess we'll be in good shape.'

And she knew that the shorter a time she had to think about things the better. The sooner the auction was over and the house was sold, the easier it would be. Then Simon would have no reason to come back to Summerset, and Jaymie could start putting her life back together again. She would have no excuse to think of him.

As if, she thought, I needed an excuse.

'And the house?' Herbert asked.

'I'm afraid that's going to take longer. I turned down another offer yesterday.'

Herbert tugged thoughtfully at his lower lip and looked concerned. 'I wish you'd let me know.'

'It didn't occur to me to call you. Should I have?'

He looked as if he was debating the point, but he finally said, 'Technically, you needn't. But it might not be a bad idea, Jaymie.'

'I'm sure you'd have agreed, because the price is still well below what we're asking. It's the same buyer—Knox Associates, the one who wants to tear it down. I don't think he'll go much higher, because the land alone can't be worth what I'm asking him to pay.' She added gloomily, 'At least I hope that's what happens.'

'So what's next? Do we wait for that young, growing family I was talking about?'

'I hope so.'

'Well, don't get impatient. With a little time, anything might happen... Of course, if you're anxious to have the whole thing settled and out of your hair...'

'I am, actually,' Jaymie admitted. 'But if you're going to suggest we put the house itself up for auction, I don't think that's such a good idea.'

'No, no. Simon suggested that instead of holding everything up until the house sells—which I agree with you could stretch into months—he could buy it from the estate.'

Jaymie blinked. 'He wants....? You're joking.'

'It's very practical, really. He's just shifting money for property, and since he's the only heir...'

'He gets it back anyway. Or most of it.'

Herbert nodded.

'So what's the point?'

'That way, you'd have all the cash necessary to settle the taxes, so, with the auction over and the paperwork done, the estate can be formally closed the day the law allows.'

Jaymie looked at him through narrowed eyes. 'What's Simon going to do with the house?'

'I assume he intends to leave it on the market and wait for an appropriate buyer. That way even if a few months elapse the estate isn't dragging out——'

'But isn't he taking a chance on losing a bundle? I mean, we've put a value on the house, but there's no guarantee it will sell for that. If he pays that amount in order to settle the estate, and then has to sell it for less——'

Herbert gave a dry little cough. 'I believe Simon has considered that possibility and decided he can afford to take the chance.'

What a very tactful way to put it, Jaymie thought almost admiringly. She wondered how much Herbert knew about the pizza king's business interests, and just when he'd found out.

She could see Simon's point, of course. He was anxious to have this mess behind him, so anxious that he would consider any possible way to get out of it. This was a pretty logical escape, all things considered, for Simon could certainly afford to take the kind of risk which was involved. All he would be gambling was money.

And money obviously held little importance to him compared to the bother of dealing with Jaymie for another few months.

She felt as if her heart was being scraped raw.

CHAPTER NINE

JAYMIE tried to reason with herself. The house was a sizeable part of Simon's inheritance; no matter what the fine print of Gretta's will had said, Jaymie's common sense told her she couldn't honestly stand in his way if he wanted to take possession of it. It wouldn't be fair, or just, or right. And in any case, what difference did it make whether she sold the property to the highest bidder or Simon did? The result would be the same.

She frowned. *The result would be the same.* So why was he so anxious to get hold of it, anyway? Jaymie was tired of the tension between them, too, but she wasn't jumping at crazy options just to get things settled a bit earlier. Nothing was going to change in the next few weeks...

But there was one thing which could, Jaymie reflected. She had told Herbert herself just a few minutes ago that she believed their most persistent bidder was about to drop out of the market. She was relieved; it meant that at least for the time being the house would survive.

But if Simon was determined to make that deal, and he saw the possibility slipping away because Jaymie was holding out for a higher price than the buyer was willing to pay...

Why should Simon care what the price was, really? He didn't need the money; a quick sale was much more of an attraction to him. But if the only way to make the deal was to get Jaymie out of the way, then this was the most sensible way to do it.

Grab the offer, she told herself. Cut yourself loose, before the pain grows even worse. At least then you won't be responsible.

But Gretta had trusted her. Gretta had purposefully, deliberately chosen Jaymie—knowing she would see the showcase through, believing she would preserve the house Gretta had loved so much. Jaymie knew now that she might not be able to do that. But she had to try, not give up like a coward.

'After the tours are over, I'll consider it,' she heard herself say. 'Until then—well, I'd feel better about leaving things as they are.'

Herbert nodded understandingly. 'You think it over,' he advised. 'And in the meantime if there are other offers, ones that come closer to the right terms, perhaps you'll let me take a look before you decide? You have every right to make the decision, of course, but it isn't quite sensible not to take legal advice, Jaymie.'

'Of course. Sorry, Herbert, I just didn't think about calling you.'

He smiled warmly and patted her shoulder and went away.

After he left, Jaymie went back to work on the curtains, tugging at each panel till it was precisely in place. Then she started unpacking the accents she had chosen—cheerful trivets, a set of antique Mason jars filled with dry pasta of various shapes and colors, and rugs and towels which picked up the bright colors in the curtains.

Holly appeared. 'Would you believe that Gloria hasn't finished the Ideal Child's room *yet*?'

'Well, I'm not done with the guest room, either.'

'Of course not. You can't do anything more till the wallpaper's finished. But nobody's even working in the child's room, and the opening party is just around the corner.'

'Don't panic. It'll be done if I have to finish it myself.'

Holly put an arm about Jaymie's shoulders. 'Sorry. It isn't fair of me to dump on you, when you're already looking like a zombie these days.'

'Thanks,' Jaymie said mildly. 'That makes me feel so much better.'

Holly laughed. 'Now I'm really sorry! What do you think of the idea of escaping all this? Once the tours are under way, let's go to St Louis for a couple of days and shop and eat and relax.'

St Louis? With my luck, Jaymie thought, I'd walk straight into Simon in the most unlikely spot in town!

'Why the disbelieving look? You don't want to let someone else have the fun of keeping all this in order?' Holly guessed.

Jaymie tried to pull herself together. The last thing she needed was for Holly to start asking questions. 'Oh, it's not that. They might realize how much work it is, and then nobody'd volunteer to take over for us next year.'

'Good point. Well, we'll finish out our obligation and after the tours we'll go celebrate. You know, I like how this kitchen turned out. Maybe the golden oak I thought I wanted wasn't such a good idea after all.'

Jaymie turned an eager face to her. 'Do you mean you still want the house, Holly? You hadn't said anything for so long I thought you'd forgotten about it, or weren't really serious.'

'I didn't bring it up because when I asked George he said he's moved for the last time and he intends to die on Park Street. I told him that could be arranged in time for me to move alone, but he didn't take me seriously.' The laughter in her voice died as she saw Jaymie's expression. 'I'm sorry, darling. I thought you'd forgotten all about it, or I'd have told you.'

Jaymie bit her lip. 'It doesn't matter. It's just that I want so badly to see it survive, and I know you'd take good care of it.'

'It makes my blood boil, too, whenever I think of that clown wanting to tear the place down after all the work we've put into it. Why don't you buy it yourself, Jaymie?'

'Me?' Jaymie tried to laugh. 'And what would I do with it?'

'Oh, I know you don't want loads of showroom space, but a little more wouldn't hurt a bit. And you could live upstairs. You could have a real office, for a change——'

'I like my office.'

'And just think, you wouldn't have to move Gretta's bedroom furniture.'

Jaymie groaned. 'Thanks for reminding me. I still haven't found a place to store it.'

'Relax—you've got another few weeks.' Holly moved to allow Jaymie to rearrange the copper pots hanging from the old wrought-iron rack above the range. 'What are you wearing to Simon's party?'

A pot almost slipped through Jaymie's hands. Simon's party? Then he *was* coming back. Why hadn't Rob known about that? 'What party?' she said coolly.

'Is he having more than one? I'm only invited to dinner Friday—before the official opening. He said it wouldn't be as elegant as he'd like, since it has to be early so the drinks and dessert affair can go on as scheduled. But since everyone he wanted to invite already had tickets to the opening, they'll be here anyway, and it was the one time he could get them all together.' Holly sighed. 'I'm not sure if I should wear beads and sequins or something less formal. But of course I can whip on an apron if I'm needed in the kitchen to serve desserts, so...'

'You might as well dress up and leave the kitchen detail to me, since I haven't been invited to the party.'

Holly stared. 'Of course you're invited.' She looked over Jaymie's shoulder. 'Isn't she?'

Before she turned around, Jaymie could feel Simon's presence. It was like a change in air pressure which made it hard to breathe and caused an ache deep in her bones...

He looked wonderful. Or was that just because she hadn't seen him for days, and her eyes were soaking up the sight? Actually, she realized, his face was thinner, even more finely honed. Had he been working hard, or not sleeping? There was an intensity in his emerald eyes that made her jittery. Had he missed her—or was she being a fool even to think he might have?

'Of course you're invited,' Simon said. He moved across the kitchen, unzipping his leather jacket. 'I could hardly leave an invitation posted on the refrigerator door for everyone to see, so I thought I'd let you have a chance to cool off for a while.'

'That's just great,' Jaymie said irritably. 'Now if I don't go it looks as if I'm in the wrong and cutting you cold!'

Holly's eyebrows had soared. 'Well,' she said finally. 'I'm glad that's all taken care of. If you'll excuse me, I'm going to call Gloria and tell her if she doesn't get to work on the Ideal Child's room today I'll lock her in the basement on bread and water.'

The silence in the kitchen was almost more than Jaymie could bear; it was like a weight pressing down on her. She didn't look at Simon, but she knew he'd moved a little closer and was leaning on the counter-top watching her.

'You don't have to ask me to the party just because Holly thinks I should be there,' she said.

'Don't be silly.' His voice was almost curt. Jaymie found his abruptness almost reassuring in a backward kind of way, until he added, 'I've been around Summerset long enough to realize what people would say if you weren't there.'

'Gee, thanks. What an honor it is to be invited!'

'Jaymie—look, I'm sorry. But it's true, you know.'

She couldn't argue with that. Everyone in Summerset would be speculating about exactly what sort of fight they'd had and whether they were likely to make up. And once that sort of question started there wasn't any end to it. Not for her, at least—since she had to live in this town. She nodded finally. 'I'll be there.'

'Friday, six o'clock, here at the house. And Jaymie...'

'What?'

'Herbert told me there are some things of Gretta's you'd like to have.'

Jaymie raised her eyebrows. 'You've already talked to him? What a coincidence.'

'I ran into him in the driveway. If you'll give me a list, Jaymie...'

She shrugged. 'Anything I want I'll buy on the auction, if it doesn't go for too high a price.'

'Surely we can come to some arrangement.'

'A swap of sorts, you mean? What do I have to do in return? Turn the house over to you?'

He paused a moment and then said gently, 'Why didn't you agree to it, Jaymie?'

'I didn't say I wouldn't,' she countered. 'I said I wanted to wait till the tours are over before I decided.'

'Why? Do you think I'd be so heartless as to cancel them?'

She shrugged. 'What are you going to do with the house, Simon? And why do you want it so badly, anyway? You don't seem the sort to want a summer home around here.'

Simon sighed. 'I don't. And I'd rather not explain right now why I want it.'

'Oh, I can understand that. Explanations aren't exactly your strong point, are they?'

'Dammit, Jaymie——' He stopped. 'Maybe I just think I can do better with it than you're doing.'

'Got a private deal in mind, hmm?'

'As a matter of fact, yes. But as things stand my hands are tied. I don't like that.'

'You don't trust me, do you, Simon?'

She expected him to pass the question off, to say, perhaps, that at least he didn't *distrust* her. But he didn't say anything at all. She could see the answer in his eyes, and the sharpness of his doubts shocked her so much that she had to turn away.

Once, she would happily have entrusted her life to him. Now there was no faith at all in her heart, and obviously none in his. There was nothing left at all, in fact, but hurt.

The caterers' vans had blocked the drive, so Jaymie came in the front door. Perhaps it was the different perspective—she hadn't used the main entrance in days—or the fact that she was dressed up for the first time in what seemed forever, but the Chadwick mansion felt like an entirely different house. Simon's party would start in half an hour, and wonderful smells were already drifting from the kitchen.

How Gretta would have loved this party, Jaymie thought. She'd have been trying to be everywhere at once...

The first sharpness of her grief was beginning to settle into a dull heartache whenever she thought of Gretta, a heartache that would diminish only with the years, and which would eventually balance out against all the delightful memories she carried. But tonight it was still painful to look around Gretta's house and feel the emptiness.

Holly, wearing a beaded cocktail dress, was setting up a small table by the front door for the ticket-takers to use when the dessert party got under way later. She looked up as Jaymie hung her wool cape in the hall closet. 'Nice dress. New?'

'No, as a matter of fact it's genuinely old.' Jaymie caught a glimpse of herself in the mirrored coat rack. As she turned, the black velvet skirt rustled, and the organdy sleeves—so lightweight that a breath could move them—flared out and then settled softly around her wrists again. 'I thought it was appropriate, since it must date from the thirties.' She jumped as the sound of hammer-blows reverberated from upstairs.

Holly gritted her teeth. 'If I go up there, I'll kill somebody.'

'Then don't. I'll take care of it. I want to make a final tour to make sure everything's in place, anyway.' A fusillade of hammer-blows escorted Jaymie up the stairs.

The guest room was all Jaymie had dreamed it would be, right down to the big jar of bright-colored marbles on the mantel. The painting was a perfect focal point. Perhaps if she bought it... But there wasn't any point; the painting was a part of this room, and she couldn't reconstruct it in some other house. In any case, she wouldn't want to try, for this room held far too many memories of Simon, and the time when she had thought in her innocence that she might be as special to him as he was to her.

That grief was more overwhelming, in a way, than the loss she felt over Gretta's death. She would have to face

Simon again tonight, and that would be like losing her hopes all over again.

She closed the door and went on down the hall to the nursery. She stood in the doorway, wanting to go in and yet afraid of what longings the room might awaken in her. Ever since Herbert had made that remark about a young and growing family she'd been catching herself dreaming—when she wasn't thinking of Simon—about babies.

She had left the Ideal Child's room for last. Not only were the two workmen still there, but also the decorator, looking harried. 'Don't say it,' Gloria begged when Jaymie looked in. 'I know I should be done by now, but honestly I'm down to the finishing touches. Another couple of hours...'

Jaymie checked the antique watch pinned to her shoulder. 'There will be dinner guests downstairs in twenty minutes.' But she couldn't help being sympathetic; if it hadn't been for Simon's help, she'd probably be in the same boat tonight.

'No more hammering,' Gloria promised. 'And I'll sneak out the back way when I'm done.'

A waitress was carrying a bar tray into the parlor as Jaymie came down the stairs, and from the dining-room she could hear the muted rattle of china.

This must be what the house was like in its prime, in the days of live-in help and seven-course meals, when the Chadwicks were the premier family of Summerset and the house was the center of the town's culture, she mused. Would it ever fill that role again, she wondered, or was tonight a last gasp of grandeur?

Simon was in the library, lounging in one of the deep leather chairs with his eyes closed and his feet propped on the big square hassock she'd brought in to serve as a coffee-table. He looked so natural there that for a moment Jaymie thought she'd conjured him up out of her own wishes, and the secret knowledge that she had thought of him every minute she'd worked in this room.

He heard her and opened his eyes, and then she couldn't just back out. 'How you can take a nap with all this bustle going on...'

'Easily,' he said, and stood up. His tuxedo was faultless, except for the lack of a tie. 'This is a very restful room, Jaymie. I congratulate you.'

She blinked and bit her lip. 'Oh. Well, thank you.'

I did it for you, she wanted to say. But that would be foolish. He couldn't care less.

He pulled his tie from his pocket and formed it into a perfect bow. An impressive performance, Jaymie conceded; not many men could do that without a mirror. But Simon didn't even seem to be thinking about it; he was watching her, studying her hair, her face, her dress.

He took two slow steps toward her. 'You were right, Jaymie. The House of Dreams is beautiful, and the showcase will be a great success.'

Jaymie had to swallow hard to hold back the tears, and even then it was difficult to talk. 'I didn't ever thank you for stripping the rest of the wallpaper upstairs. I'd never have made it without your help.'

Simon didn't answer, and Jaymie looked up at him for an instant through her lashes. He was so close that she could see her face reflected in the shiny silver studs in his shirt.

If he kissed her now, she wondered, would it make a difference? Would it help them bridge the gulf of mistrust which lay between them? Or would it only make things hurt worse?

His fingertips brushed against her hair, and Jaymie almost panicked. She heard the murmur of voices from the hall and seized on the sound as if it were a life raft.

'Your guests are starting to arrive, Simon.' And you're a chicken, Jaymie Logan, she told herself.

He didn't answer, simply offered his arm—so they went out together to greet his guests. The people who, if things had been different, could have been *their* guests...

But things weren't different, she reminded herself. And it was only her imagination which said they could have been.

The caterers had gone, leaving the lingering scents of beef Wellington and citrus salad dressing permeating the kitchen. The dozens of elaborate desserts had been cut and served and eaten and exclaimed over. And the first tours had been a hit as well.

Simon was still in the foyer saying goodnight to the last of the party-goers when Jaymie retreated to the kitchen. The caterers had cleaned up after themselves; the room was spotless and all the dishes were washed, but the dining-room table had to be set up once more before the house would be ready for tomorrow's tours. Half an hour, she promised herself, and the last of her work would be done.

Quiet gradually settled over the house. She wondered if Simon had gone as well, and wondered where he was headed. She had half expected that he would be leaving Summerset again tomorrow, but she'd overheard him saying goodnight to her parents as if he didn't intend to go back to the Logan house at all. That surprised her, for it was almost midnight—hardly a reasonable hour to start out.

She worked quickly and quietly—setting out china, folding fresh napkins, arranging flatware—and was startled when someone knocked at the back door. At this hour, who could possibly have an errand here? Holly, perhaps, coming back to give her a hand?

But it was Gloria who stood at the door, shivering in the April wind, still dressed in the work clothes she'd been wearing earlier when Jaymie had found her working frantically to finish the Ideal Child's room. 'Did you come to make sure I get the dining-room put together right?'

Gloria shook her head. 'I don't care,' she said. 'I came to retrieve my tools. I stuck them in the closet because I was cutting it so close I didn't even have time to carry them out.'

'I didn't think I saw you at the party.'

Gloria rolled her eyes. 'Party? I barely made it out the door before it started, and I certainly didn't have the energy to change clothes and celebrate.' She headed for the stairs. 'Next time you get a brainstorm for a showcase house, Jaymie, leave me out, all right?'

Jaymie went back to the dining-room and surveyed the table once more. There were a couple of water-spotted crystal goblets, but other than that...

Gloria hardly had time to climb the stairs before Jaymie heard her coming down once more. This time her footsteps were loud and fast and forceful, and she was breathing hard as she came into the dining-room. Jaymie looked up in astonishment. Gloria was not carrying any tools, and she looked like a madwoman— her eyes were wild and her hair was standing almost on end, as if she'd run her fingers through it in frustration. Gloria was a melodramatic type, that was true—but Jaymie had never seen her look like this before.

'That tears it,' Gloria said through clenched teeth.

'What happened?'

'The whole damned thing is falling apart, that's what. This stupid showcase has been a thankless chore from the beginning, and now that whole room is a complete wreck. I quit. Since you have so many good ideas, Jaymie, you can help yourself if you want, but I'm done. I'm finished. That's it!'

She slammed the door between the dining-room and the kitchen, and the crystal goblets shivered in sympathetic vibration.

Jaymie looked up as if she could see through the ceiling and into the Ideal Child's room directly above. Then, fearfully, she climbed the stairs as fast as her narrow velvet skirt allowed.

At first glance, the room looked undisturbed, and for a split-second she wondered what had upset Gloria so. The loft bed stood straight and sturdy. The bookshelves hadn't collapsed. The floor hadn't caved in.

Then she saw the far corner, almost blocked from view by the bulk of the loft bed. The wallpaper—the new, expensive, heavy paper which had just been installed yesterday—had begun to peel away from the wall, ripping from its own weight as it sagged. Worse, it had pulled down pieces of the ceiling as well; chunks of fallen plaster were scattered over the carpet.

No wonder Gloria had reacted so strongly. There was no easy fix for a problem like this. The wallpaper had stretched and twisted as it tore; there was no way to put it back in place. And as for the ceiling—if parts of it had failed with so little stress, the adjoining areas were likely to be weak as well. The only real solution to that problem was to knock down all the loose plaster and start over.

But, of course, there was no time for major construction. Tomorrow morning at nine, people would start knocking at the front door, presenting their tickets, expecting to see a finished house—a showcase—not a renovation still in progress.

Jaymie backed up into the doorway—as if, she thought, not seeing the mess would make it go away!—and bumped into something warm and firm. She gave a shriek and spun around.

Simon's arms closed about her, taking the weight off her suddenly shaky knees. She would have pushed herself away, but she wasn't certain she could stand on her own. 'Where did you come from?' she gasped.

'The library.' He was looking over her head at the wreckage. 'I heard the uproar. What happened?'

Jaymie turned toward the room again. 'Remember what I told you about the terrible results when you put new wallpaper on without stripping off the old?'

'This is it? I see.'

'I was so far behind schedule myself that I didn't realize Gloria was cutting corners. But that's what she must have done, because you can see the old paper under the torn edges of the new.'

Abruptly she realized that she was still leaning against Simon, her spine fitted neatly against his chest, his arms folded around her waist, his breath stirring her hair. She closed her eyes for a second and savored the feeling of being so close to him. It was a crazy mixture of comfort and excitement. She had a sensation of warmth and peace, as if she was safe so long as she stayed close to him. But at the same time her body was alight with delicious danger because of that selfsame closeness...

With determination she took a step away. Simon let her go and crossed the room to look more closely at the damage. 'What now? Can you stick it back up?'

She shook her head. 'Industrial-strength glue might hold it in place, but the tears would show. I suppose we'll just have to close the room. It's a shame, since the furniture is so darling, but——'

'Can't you cover it with something else?'

'Like what? An old sheet? Wouldn't that look just great?' Jaymie pressed her palms to her temples. 'Wait a minute, you might have something there after all. It's worth a try.'

Her narrow skirt was a handicap on the twisting stairs to the tower room, and despite her head start Simon was right behind her when she reached the top. She took one startled look around. 'No wonder you couldn't get comfortable up here,' she muttered, and started tugging boxes out of the way. 'They're here somewhere; they've got to be.'

'If you'll tell me what you're looking for, I'll help.'

'The old green drapes from the living-room. They were in such bad shape when Rob took them down that he wanted to throw them away, but they're brocade, and I thought there might be enough good pieces to cover a footstool or something.'

They had to shift nearly everything in the room before she found the drapes, rolled into an untidy wad in the far corner.

'So now that we've got this treasure, what do we do with it?' Simon said, looking at their find—and the dust on his tuxedo—with distaste.

'We're going to make the damaged corner into a soft-sculpture tree.'

Simon looked at her for a long moment. 'Of course,' he said solemnly. 'I knew that. I just wanted to be sure you agreed it was the right thing to do.'

Jaymie smiled just a little. 'Since it's already a loft, why not make it a tree house as well?' She shook out the brocade panels and nodded. 'I think there's just enough. Look for something brownish for the trunk, all right? I'm going to see if Gloria left a staple gun and a pair of scissors.'

A few minutes later Simon came back to the bedroom. 'One antique brown tweed man's suit,' he said. 'No doubt moth-eaten.'

Jaymie held it up. 'That will do.' Briskly, she sliced the suit's seams and started stapling the pieces to the plaster, stretching the fabric across the corner to form a trunk and arching branches up the walls.

Simon took the staple gun out of her hand. 'Let me do that.'

Within minutes a tree began to form, as puffy and round and cartoonish as a kindergartner's drawing, looking as if it had grown right up the corner of the room.

Jaymie tried to concentrate on the tree and not think about how easily they were working together, almost as if they were of one mind. She could almost pretend that the last week of tension had never existed, that they were back in the guest room on that wonderful afternoon when they had stripped wallpaper and talked and shared their feelings...

I thought we shared, she reminded herself. But we didn't.

Even Simon had trouble reaching the highest corners, but eventually the tree was finished.

'Thanks for sticking around to help with this,' she said finally. 'I know you must be anxious to go...'

'Who said I was going anywhere?'

Relief licked at Jaymie's heart for an instant and then faded. 'Dad did, when he told you goodbye tonight.'

'Oh. I guess he did, in a way. I thought I'd imposed on Van and Carla long enough, so I've moved to the hotel. The staff down there is used to people coming and going, and until I get a few things sorted out it wasn't fair to your mother to use her house like Grand Central Station.'

'A few things sorted out', she thought. Things like what would happen to the house? She still hadn't agreed to let him buy it from the estate, but once the tours were over she wouldn't be able to delay things any more.

'You do a lot of that, don't you?' It was an idle comment, not really a question at all. 'Coming and going, I mean. Are you looking for a new project?'

'Of course. I need a new challenge. That's really why I sold the pizza chain—because all the excitement had gone out of it. But I have to do something with all the time I used to spend clearing tables and mopping floors.'

'Is that what's taking you to St Louis all the time?'

He nodded. 'And points beyond.'

Well, she hadn't expected details, had she? He'd never volunteered that kind of thing, and he certainly didn't owe them to her now.

Jaymie stepped back to take a critical look at the tree. 'I think we're going to get by with it. Anybody who hasn't already had the tour won't even wonder why it's here.'

'Oh, it's a very credible tree,' he agreed.

The cynical note in his voice made her ask, 'But you're thinking of what's underneath, aren't you?'

'Camouflaging problems doesn't make them go away.'

'It's just plaster, Simon. It's nothing serious like a cracked foundation or termites in the attic. And if you think this is going to make me agree that the house should be torn down——'

'Dammit, Jaymie, if you'd only *listen*——' He set the stapler down on the green brocade and pulled the trigger as if in emphasis.

Jaymie felt the staple graze her fingertip. Reflexively, she pulled away and stuck her finger in her mouth. 'Simon, would you watch what you're doing with that thing?'

Simon dropped the stapler and seized her hand. 'Are you all right?'

'Only by pure luck.'

'I'm sorry, sweetheart.' He kissed the almost injured fingertip, then cupped her palm against his face. His tongue traced her lifeline, and lightning exploded throughout Jaymie's body.

She turned her head and found herself staring straight into Simon's eyes. His hand slipped to the nape of her neck and drew her toward him, and his lips came to rest on hers with an urgent demand which was equalled by her own longing.

Every cell of Jaymie's body was aflame. Any common sense she'd ever possessed was burning up, too, but she didn't care about that at the moment. She wanted only to be kissed like this forever...

Then Simon whispered, 'Jaymie, sweetheart, why won't you just stop fighting me?'

Because I can't give up wanting you, she thought, and faced the fact that it wasn't the house she had been trying to protect when she had refused to go along with his plan. She had been shielding the last fragments of hope that something could still grow between them. She had been trying to hold onto Simon. And only now, when he had kissed her not with caring but with calculation, could she see that the outcome was inevitable. And she must stop trying, or she would break herself to bits in the effort. For her own sake, it was time to give up and do as he had asked—stop fighting.

'All right,' she said. Her voice was shaking. 'Tomorrow I'll tell Herbert to draw up the papers, and just as soon as that's done you'll have your house, and you can do whatever you want with it.'

'Jaymie——'

She put both hands on his chest and pushed. 'I just want this to be over.' Then she turned and walked away, and left him standing there.

CHAPTER TEN

THE auction was to start at ten in the morning, but the sales crews must have begun work at dawn, for when Jaymie arrived the front lawn was already lined with furniture and tables full of knickknacks and china. The bookkeeper's booth was set up in the driveway, and a concessions tent was doing a booming business selling coffee and doughnuts.

It was a perfect April morning, and prospective bidders were already wandering over the grounds, inspecting the merchandise and assessing the competition. Jaymie nodded and smiled at a couple she recognized as dealers from the next town. At this rate, the Chadwick auction would be the biggest of the season.

Two of the auctioneers' men came down the porch steps carrying the *chaise-longue* from the guest room and set it down at the end of the row, almost at Jaymie's feet. She smiled a little as she remembered the morning she'd found Simon asleep on that couch in the solarium. It would be a whole lot more comfortable now, with new springs and a fresh, crisp cover...

She caught herself caressing the spot on the couch's back where his head had rested and pulled her hand away as if she'd been burned. The day would be painful enough as it was, having to watch the things Gretta had loved and lived with dispersed to the four points of the compass, without thinking of Simon and the way she wished things had been.

Rob had told her Simon was still going back and forth to St Louis—and, she supposed, to those mysterious points beyond he'd mentioned. Jaymie didn't know where he found time, for it seemed that everywhere she turned she ran into him. Twice she'd encountered him at her parents' house, where he'd been drinking coffee and talking to Van. Once she'd seen him on the front porch of the Chadwick mansion, chatting with a woman who'd later turned up on a tour Jaymie was conducting. Once he'd dipped an ice-cream cone for her at Millers' and paid for it himself.

And only last week he'd been walking through the gardens around the house just as Jaymie was leaving after her regular stint as a guide. She didn't even know if he'd seen her that day; he'd been so busy talking to the two men who were with him that he hadn't even looked up. She hadn't recognized the men, so she was relatively sure they weren't part of Knox Associates. But of course that didn't mean much.

One thing had been obvious, though; all three of them had seemed far more interested in the landscape than anything else. She wondered if they'd even bothered to look at the house, or if they were condemning it sight unseen.

But of course that wasn't her concern any more. The day after the party, when she'd told Simon she would agree to whatever he wanted, Herbert had turned up with a sheaf of papers for Jaymie to sign. And so, no matter what happened to the house, it was none of Jaymie's business.

She bumped into another early bird, apologized, and reminded herself that she was not going to spend today dwelling on what might happen to the house. She was not going to think about Simon, either. She'd think instead of the things she wanted to buy for herself.

Her list was a short one—just those few possessions of Gretta's that she'd told Herbert she'd like to have.

Some bits of crystal, some china, a few small items of furniture. She hoped she had enough money set aside to buy them. With a crowd like this prices could go high.

But perhaps that was just as well. Heaven knew she didn't need concrete reminders; she had memories enough to fill the days and months ahead. Pleasant memories of Gretta—and less pleasant ones of Simon.

The two men carried out the guest room daybed and set it down almost in front of Jaymie. As she side-stepped to avoid it she bumped into a woman who was coming up to look at the couch.

The woman smiled politely and turned away to run a hand across the back of the *chaise*. Jaymie recognized her—mostly because she was the one who'd been talking to Simon on the front porch a few days ago. But she'd stood out in other ways as well. She'd been alone, while most showcase visitors arrived in groups, and she hadn't said a word through the whole tour—not an exclamation, not a question, not a comment about doing something differently.

'Jaymie!' Holly was making her way through the growing crowd, waving a slip of paper. 'Look at this!'

'Hold it still so I can see.' Jaymie took one look and blinked in surprise at a personal check, written in a strong hand in very black ink, for thirty thousand dollars—signed by Simon Nichols. 'What's that all about?'

'Simon asked me this morning what I thought the redecoration would have cost in normal circumstances, and off the top of my head I told him twenty thousand.'

'You're way low,' Jaymie said.

'That's exactly what he said. Then he pulled out his checkbook and started writing. Why didn't you tell me Simon could afford gestures like this?'

Jaymie avoided the question. 'Maybe he's sold the house.' Just saying the words hurt.

Deliberately, she forced herself to think it through. Perhaps he'd gotten more money than he'd expected to. If so, he might actually have come to believe her original promise that redecorating would add value, and he felt that the Service League should benefit too. She supposed she should feel vindicated, but it didn't seem to make a difference any more.

Though as a matter of fact she thought it very unlikely that the kind of buyers Simon was going after would have paid more because of wallpaper and curtains. More likely, Simon simply felt guilty that all their hard work would soon be gone forever. What better way to silence his conscience than to give a lot of money to a very good cause?

'I don't know. Krista won't say anything specific, of course, but I know she's showed a lot of people through, and she's taken him a couple of offers.' Holly held the check up for inspection. 'In any case, no matter what inspired him to do it, our charities are going to have a plum of a year, aren't they?'

'And you'll go out of office looking like a saint.'

'Saint Holly... I could get used to the sound of that.'

The crowd was gathering around the porch; the auctioneer stood on the steps with his portable microphone, making the standard announcements about the terms of the sale. Then he swung into the sing-song patter which was almost like another language. It took a few minutes for Jaymie's ears to adjust to the lingo, and by then he was selling the first of the items she wanted—a box of old Havilland china. She put the first bid on it and thought for a moment that the crowd was going to let her have it uncontested. Then from across the crowd a second voice sang out, and the race was on. Finally, Jaymie shook her head in frustration and dropped out.

'But if you want the china...' Holly argued.

'Honey, the first rule of auctions is to set a price beforehand, while you're still level-headed, and stick to it. Otherwise, once you get the fever no amount of money seems too much.' Jaymie looked up just in time to catch the final price, and the woman who had been looking at the *chaise-longue* held up her bidding number for the clerk to note.

'That's a lot of money for a few dishes,' Holly said.

'See what I mean?' Jaymie looked over the lawn. Even at the brisk pace the auctioneer had set, it was going to take hours to move through all the merchandise.

She had half expected that at the last minute Simon would change his mind and hold back a few things for himself, but it didn't seem as if that had happened. Didn't the man have a single sentimental bone in his body? It seemed the only things he'd really wanted were the family pictures and albums.

She saw Bess at the far side of the lawn, away from the bidding action. She looked a great deal older than she had the day of Gretta's funeral, and Jaymie's heart ached. Bess had lost a good friend and her home in one blow, and no pension could make up for that. Jaymie started across the crowd toward her.

A hand reached out and clutched her arm; Jaymie turned around to confront an enormous lampshade, one of the most recent items to have been sold. From behind it peered a member of the local theater group. 'Jaymie, I've got a tremendous favor to ask,' she said eagerly. 'Can we borrow the house two weeks from Saturday night? We want to have a murder-mystery party as a fund-raiser, and it would be perfect.'

'It's not up to me. You can ask Simon, but——' Jaymie had to bite her tongue to keep from saying 'in a couple of weeks the whole place might be dust'. 'Besides, with no furniture——'

'Oh, the setting's supposed to be an abandoned mansion. It'll be an adventure. In case I can't get close to Simon today, would you ask him?'

'If I have the chance,' Jaymie said finally.

'And if you want to come to the party, I've got tickets. You'd both love it.'

That was all she needed, Jaymie thought—for Summerset to start thinking of her and Simon as a couple, long after any possibility of that was gone.

She couldn't see Bess any more; the woman was so tiny that she had vanished into the crowd. So Jaymie made her way back the few feet to Holly's side and watched the sale for a while.

She bid on a couple of items, without much success. The woman who'd bought the Havilland china also ended up with the pair of leather chairs from the library, she noticed. Jaymie got Gretta's pottery breakfast set for a song, though she gave up on the set of crystal goblets when they went far above her budget. She watched the rest of the bidding, though, and was surprised when the same woman bought those as well.

'She must be a dealer,' Holly said.

Jaymie shrugged. 'Maybe, but I don't know how she expects to make a profit, considering the prices she's paying.'

'Perhaps you're right about Simon selling the house, and she's the one who bought it. The way she's spending money, no wonder he had an extra thirty thousand for us.'

Jaymie started to shake her head, and then frowned instead, watching as the woman, in quick succession, bought the *chaise-longue* and the daybed from the guest room. She was certainly buying a lot of the important furniture. If she hadn't bought the Chadwick house, she seemed intent on re-creating it. And if she had—well,

Holly might be right. From the way the woman was bidding, price was no object.

'Though when I think about it,' Holly went on, 'maybe not. George told me he saw your dad and Simon having lunch with a contractor the other day.'

Then he's still negotiating that offer, Jaymie thought, and frowned. Why would her father have been involved in that sort of deal? Van Logan was gung ho for all sorts of new development, of course—that was his job. But he typically wasn't insensitive about local history. He wouldn't lightly approve the loss of a landmark like the Chadwick mansion. And why would he be involved in Simon's negotiations, anyway?

Jaymie shrugged off the question. 'Was it Knox Associates?'

Holly shook her head. 'No. I can't remember the name, but George told me it was the guy who's building the town houses out in Paradise Valley. George said they were all so busy sketching on the placemats that they hardly saw him.'

Every muscle in Jaymie's body tensed. It didn't make sense for Simon to be dealing with a different contractor all of a sudden. Had the deal with Knox fallen through after all?

And why would Simon bother with sketches, anyway? He'd pointed out himself that it wouldn't be any of his business what the next owner did with it—whether it was apartments, town houses or something else altogether. As long as they met his price...

Then the pieces clicked into place in her brain. The unknown men she'd seen looking over the property with him and the conversations she'd walked into between Simon and her father had a new significance—especially when she put it all together with what Van had said that first night at dinner about Summerset's housing shortage and the fortune that could be made from it. Only a casual comment, she'd thought at the time—but Simon hadn't forgotten it, for he'd brought it up again the day Krista had brought that first offer from Knox Associates.

'Maybe I just think I can do better with it than you're doing,' he'd said. She'd thought he meant only money, but now the words held a new significance.

Jaymie took a deep breath, trying to clear her head. No wonder Simon had wanted to get the property in his own name, she thought. It wasn't a matter of convenience or avoiding delay, it was sheer necessity—for he didn't intend to sell the house, or the valuable land it sat on. He was going to destroy it himself, and build anew.

There was no reason on earth why he shouldn't, of course. The land and the house were his now. The project even made a convoluted, tragic sort of sense—if the house was to be destroyed anyway, why shouldn't Simon make the investment himself and reap all the profit, instead of selling only the land? He'd been looking for a new challenge; it seemed he'd found it right here in Summerset. And if he'd made her father some kind of adviser or partner...

Jaymie had suddenly lost all interest in the auction. She no longer cared whether she got the items she had been so interested in a few minutes ago. She even forgot the breakfast set, loosely stacked in a box at her feet, until she kicked the cardboard carton and dishes rattled in protest.

'You'd better be careful with that,' Holly said. 'Pottery chips so easily. Maybe you'd better pack it up—we left some extra newspapers on the back porch, I think.'

Jaymie nodded. One excuse was as good as another, and right now she just needed to be alone. 'See you later, Holly.'

'Anything you want me to bid on if it comes up while you're gone?'

Jaymie shook her head. She didn't even look at what might be coming up for sale soon. She didn't care any more.

The house was locked, but she had tucked the big, old-fashioned key into her pocket. She juggled the box of pottery as she opened the back door.

The kitchen was still and quiet. Dust motes danced in the streams of sunshine, but that was the only thing which moved. The kitchen table was gone, of course; it had been carried out for sale this morning. And all the accessories she'd arranged so carefully had been taken back to her shop.

She'd left the curtains, though. She looked up at the bright-colored puffs and almost laughed. Why had she bothered?

And why, she asked herself, was she so upset just now? She had known for weeks that the house was likely to be torn down; what difference did it make who did it?

She looked deep into her heart, and what she saw shocked her. 'Because I didn't think he'd go through with it,' she whispered.

Down deep, under it all, she had still held onto a kernel of trust, a conviction that, when the time came to sign the papers that would condemn this wonderful old house, Simon wouldn't do it. She had been certain, in the bottom of her heart, that when he faced that choice——

'You thought he'd meekly do what you wanted him to,' she accused herself. 'But why should he, Jaymie? There's nothing special about you.'

She picked up a cup and held it cradled in her hand. The temptation to throw it, to shatter the silence of the room by splintering a few dishes, was almost more than she could bear, and, afraid she would give in to the temptation, she hurried to find a couple of newspapers. The rhythmic action of packing soothed her a little.

'Everything all right in here?' Simon was at the back door.

Jaymie didn't even look up. 'Fine.'

He moved a little closer. 'Did you get the crystal you were bidding on?'

She hadn't seen him anywhere around the grounds since the auction had started, much less been aware that he was watching her. The idea sent a cold shiver down her spine, until she reminded herself that he couldn't have been paying much attention or he'd know that she hadn't prevailed on that particular bid.

She shook her head. 'It went too high.'

'I'm sorry about that. If you'd given me a list of what you wanted, I'd have made sure you got what you wanted. It's only right, since you're not even taking pay.'

Jaymie slammed a cup into a corner of the packing box and said fiercely, 'Everything I've done has been for Gretta's sake, not for money. Dammit, Simon——'

He held up both hands. 'All right. I apologize. Don't take it out on the dishes.'

She took a deep breath and dug a hand into the pocket of her jeans. 'Here's my key to the house,' she said, holding it out. 'After the auction's over, most of my work as executor is done. And now that the tours are over I won't have any need for it.'

Simon made no move to take it. 'Your furniture is still all over the place.'

'Oh.' She felt foolish. 'I'd forgotten about that.'

'Don't worry about the key. You may as well keep it as a souvenir.'

'Because that's all the good it will be—is that what you mean?'

He leaned against the counter and folded his arms across his chest. 'What's eating you, anyway?' he countered.

She shook her head. 'I guess I never really believed you'd do it, Simon.'

'Do what?'

'Please don't tear it down!' She ducked her head a little, afraid to face him with her question. 'Will you sell it to me instead? I know I can't give you what it's worth, but you can afford a grand gesture. This house doesn't deserve to die. Please, won't you let me try to save it?'

Only silence answered her, thick and harsh. Then Simon said, 'Why, Jaymie? Because it's your darling, your pet cause?'

'What if it is? It's still a wonderful place. It's more than just walls and floors, Simon—there's a magic here, made of all the memories that have soaked into this house all through the years... Oh, why would I expect you to understand?'

She didn't look at him, but she could feel the incredulity in the air. He must think she had gone completely bananas.

'Never mind,' Jaymie said stiffly. 'It's a stupid idea. This house would probably bankrupt me. Forget it.'

'I'd be tempted by the deal, but you see...I've already decided what to do with it.' Simon's voice was low, and there was a husky edge to it that she'd never heard before.

Jaymie nodded. At least I tried, she told herself, and started to turn away.

'I'm going to keep it,' he added softly.

She blinked and told herself that she was hearing strange noises. 'Yeah, right. You've been talking to a contractor—and not the sort who patches falling ceilings, either, but the kind who builds developments. So don't tell me you're not going to take advantage of the housing shortage and build——'

'Who told you that?'

'George Dermott saw you and told Holly.'

Simon sighed. 'And so you thought I was going to build an apartment complex right here? I told you I don't know anything about housing.' He added, almost to himself, 'I've got to stop underestimating Summerset's grapevine.'

'If you think you're being funny, Simon——'

'I'm sorry,' he said quickly. 'I didn't even consider what that conference might look like to an observer. But I assure you it had nothing to do with the house.'

'Just the land?'

'Not even that. I was talking to the contractor because...' He shifted nervously from one foot to the other. 'Because I bought Millers' malt shop.'

She shook her head, confused. 'What's that got to do with anything? It would hardly take a contractor to remodel the shop.'

'It's the best ice-cream I've ever tasted,' Simon said patiently, 'but nobody outside of Summerset knows about it. I think that's a shame, so I'm going to put up a factory out in that new industrial park your father's so fond of and make it commercially in large quantities.'

She stared at him for a long time. '*That's* why you were talking to the contractor? About a factory?'

'That's why. I swear it.'

She sniffed a little. 'You could have told me.' That was idiotic, she reminded herself. Why should he have thought she'd be interested?

'I've been toying with the idea since that basketball game, but we just struck the deal this week, so I wasn't exactly making announcements. It's taken a lot of research and planning——'

'All those trips to St Louis?'

'And a whole lot of other places. I've been talking to distributors, consulting manufacturers, pulling in favors from business contacts. If the product is as successful as I think it's going to be, we'll start franchising shops within the next few years, too.'

She remembered what he'd said about the pizza business, and how he'd gotten into it by buying just one restaurant with a good product and a lot of potential. 'I feel like a fool,' she whispered. 'You've been thinking of hundreds of soda fountains, and I...'

He smiled a little. 'I don't have any idea how many there might be eventually. I just know I'm not going to run them personally. I'll be staying right here in Summerset, being the Ideal Man.' He looked around. 'Right here.'

She stared at him, eyes wide. He had said he would keep the house, but she hadn't realized he meant to live in it, to make it his home. 'You wanted to keep it? But you said——'

'At first, I did want to sell it, and by the time I realized I'd changed my mind... Well, that was the moment I realized I didn't want to give it up—when you announced you'd signed the listing, and it was too late to stop you. You see, you'd said you wouldn't sell it till after the tours, so I thought I had plenty of time to think it over.'

'I thought you needed the money,' Jaymie said irritably.

'I didn't realize that. Then I tried to talk you into letting me handle all the offers.'

'So you could turn them all down? Oh, Simon——'

'But you insisted on taking care of it yourself. And, no matter what I said about the horrors of selling the house, you just got more adamant that it would be sold——'

'Is that why you went into such ghastly detail about how I couldn't control what happened to it after the sale?'

He nodded. 'The only other way to keep it safe from you was to buy it myself—so that's what I did.'

'To keep it safe from you'. From Jaymie, who had loved that house as much as it was possible to love four walls. She bit her lip hard. If that was what he honestly thought, then there was nothing left that was worth trying to save.

She put her chin up. 'Well,' she said as cheerfully as she could, 'so you're going to live here and make ice-cream. Congratulations.'

'And build birdhouses in the basement, I suppose. I draw the line at taking up the violin, though.' He smiled at her.

Jaymie thought, So this is what it feels like when a heart breaks. If he can tell me that so casually, and not even realize that I care what he does . . .

Once, she told herself, she would have started shouting with glee at the announcement that he wanted to build a life for himself in Summerset. But right now she would almost rather see the house torn down than watch him live here happily with someone else, building the Ideal Family.

'I've had to rethink my life,' Simon went on. 'Not being here when Gretta died hit me hard. She was the last of my family, but I let my business come before her.'

It was funny that in the midst of her own pain Jaymie still wanted most to soothe his. 'You couldn't have known, Simon. No one realized till too late how ill she was.'

'Yes, I could have known. I should have been in touch without Herbert's efforts to find me.'

Almost automatically she put out a hand to try to offer comfort, and then pulled back, certain that he wouldn't want her sympathy.

'I haven't had a home for years, Jaymie. I've spent a few months here, a couple of years there. But as I watched you make this house into a home, I realized how much I wanted that.'

That, he had said. Not *you*. There was a world of difference. Jaymie forced herself to smile, but her lips trembled so much that she had to turn away. 'I'm glad, Simon.'

'Are you?' he whispered. 'I hope so.'

She couldn't look at him. She stared down into the box of pottery, not seeing it, as something deep inside her twisted into a knot.

'Because, you see, if someday you'd like to share my house—my life—all those memories you spoke of...and make new ones with me...'

She spun around to face him, and the joy in her eyes made him catch his breath. 'Oh, Simon!'

He did not catch her close immediately; instead he cupped her face in his hands and just looked at her for a long moment as if she were a precious jewel.

And as he kissed her—tenderly at first, and then with rising certainty and passion—the knot inside Jaymie slowly relaxed until it was gone for good.

Simon raised his head and whispered, 'I love you so.'

Jaymie had to shake herself out of a fog in order to answer. 'Me too,' she managed. 'Simon, you don't really think I'd have let the house be torn down?'

He held her a little way from him and said soberly, 'I think at one point you were so angry and frustrated that you'd have done almost anything—tear it down, sell it to Holly...'

'That's what you meant, about saving it from me?'

He nodded.

'Oh,' she said softly. 'What about the men you were showing it to last week?'

'They're landscape architects. Didn't I tell you the garden needs a complete overhaul?'

There was no point in arguing about exactly what he'd said. So she just smiled, and he kissed her again.

It was a long time later that Simon asked, 'Do you suppose we'd better make an appearance before someone reports us missing?'

Until that moment, Jaymie had forgotten all about the auction. She spared an instant of regret for the things which were now forever gone, things which she would have liked to remain a part of the house. The very special guest room could never be re-created now.

The important thing, of course, was that they had worked it out, and they were together. Still...

'I wonder if they've sold the kitchen table yet?' she said.

'I expect so.' Simon rubbed his chin comfortably against her hair. 'They were getting close to it when I came inside.'

'Oh. I wish we'd figured all this out before the auction.'

He raised his eyebrows. 'And kept it all? We do have to have room for us, and the way Gretta had filled up this house...'

She smiled bravely. 'You're right, of course. Maybe it's better to make a whole new start. At least you've still got the family pictures.'

'And you've got a rose velvet parlor suite, and a walnut coat tree, and a Boston rocker...and don't forget the bedroom set.'

The sultry note in his voice made her think of a furry rug thrown down in front of the fireplace in the master bedroom, and two people snuggling in the warmth of a blazing fire, and a warm little thrill trembled through her body.

'Very smart of you not to find a storage place for your bedroom set,' Simon mused. 'It saves such a lot of work moving it back. And by the way, my administrative assistant is out there right now busily buying everything Herbert and I could figure out that you wanted.'

'What administrative assistant? Is that the woman I always talked to when I called you?'

'That's the one.'

'She's in Summerset? Why?'

'Because it was a nuisance to call her in Atlanta every time I wanted her to do something. And as long as we're talking of nuisances——' he gently tweaked her earlobe '—may I remind you I told you to give me a list of what you wanted?'

Jaymie wasn't listening. The woman who had bought the crystal goblets, she thought, and the *chaise-longue* and the daybed and the library chairs...

For me, she thought. She bit her lip and tried not to cry.

'She's also buying anything you started to bid on, if you dropped out before it sold, and some additions of her own, gleaned from observing you when she took the tour. I told her to buy anything you seemed to think was important—just in case someday you wanted it.'

'Simon, wouldn't it have been simpler to hold those things out of the sale?'

'And explain to you why I suddenly wanted stuff I'd never shown any interest in before? A whole houseful of stuff, at that—and the very things you liked best?' With the tip of his index finger, he traced her profile.

'I guess I see your point, but——'

'I wasn't ready to do that, Jaymie. I wasn't ready to take the risk of telling you that I'd fallen in love with you.'

She shook her head in disbelief.

'You did keep telling me things like how you couldn't wait to get finished with the estate,' he reminded her, 'and how you were only interested in seeing the showcase through. It wasn't till today, when you started talking about memories... The way you said it, I knew some of those memories had to include me, and if you were starting to think about that, then perhaps you'd realize that what we have is very special. But till then—well, if even Gretta wasn't able to make you feel a little interest in me, I wasn't about to announce that I wanted not only the house and the furniture, but you too—and take a chance on you bursting into laughter.'

Jaymie frowned. 'I don't understand.'

'Oh, please,' he groaned. 'It doesn't take a rocket scientist to figure out what Gretta had in mind. There's nothing like a never-married old lady when it comes to romantic plotting, and the Ideal Couple is just the sort of transparent, damn-fool trick Gretta would think of. But it never even occurred to you that she was talking about us, did it? And that she threw us together on purpose?'

Jaymie colored a little. 'No. I just knew that whenever the subject came up I found myself thinking about you.'

'Oh?' He sounded delighted. 'So how about it? Would you like to try being the Ideal Woman?'

'I haven't been very ideal so far,' Jaymie admitted. 'I've leaped to conclusions so often, I could be an Olympic champion.'

'That's true. But then I have to admit I'm not likely to be successful at my role all the time either. And when the Ideal Babies come along...'

Jaymie could feel soft color creeping into her face.

'I suspect we'll have to throw the script away,' Simon said. 'Gretta didn't have that one right at all. Our children could never be ordinary enough to be ideal.'

And then Jaymie couldn't say anything at all for a while. A little later, however, she drew back a bit and reminded him, 'You told Holly you were in deadly fear of me.'

Simon nodded. 'Oh, yes. I knew from the first day that you could be a danger to my peace of mind if I wasn't careful. When you stopped the will-reading to defend Bess from injustice, it occurred to me that you could be serious trouble.'

'Thanks a bunch, Simon,' she said drily. 'That's very flattering.'

'You're welcome. I did come back because of deadly fear. You see, I couldn't stop thinking about you, and I was afraid I never would. I thought at first that if I got to know you better the fascination would pass.'

'And?' Jaymie prompted.

'It didn't. It only kept getting stronger.' He rubbed his cheek against her hair. 'What shall we do about Bess, by the way? I was thinking of asking her to come back as a sort of housekeeper emeritus. You know, doing what she feels like and supervising the rest of the work.'

Jaymie nodded. 'This house is going to take a lot of keeping up... Oh, I forgot—I was supposed to ask you something. The theater group wants to use the house for a mystery party in a couple of weeks.'

'Maybe next year,' Simon said comfortably. 'But not right now. We've got a wedding to put on.'

'Now that you mention it, I had some ideas once about that...'

But as he kissed her once more, Jaymie forgot all about it. After a while, she leaned back comfortably in his arms, looked up at him and asked, 'Do you really think Gretta honestly believed all she needed to do was bring us into the same circle and a miraculous storybook sort of love would take care of the rest? That's nonsense.'

Simon kissed her temple. 'Of course it is. I'd even call it whimsical.'

'Utterly ridiculous.'

He smiled down into her eyes. 'Medieval. But nevertheless, Jaymie...it's forever, too.'

And Jaymie buried her head in his shoulder, content to take his word for it.

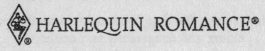 **HARLEQUIN ROMANCE®**

brings you

More Romances Celebrating Love, Families and Children!

Following on from Rosemary Gibson's *No Ties*, Harlequin Romance #3344, this month we're bringing you *A Valentine for Daisy*, Harlequin Romance #3347, which we know you will enjoy reading! It's a wonderful Betty Neels story, all about two adorable twins Josh and Katie who play their part in Daisy finding true love at last!

Watch out for these titles:

KIDSG9

Where do you find hot Texas nights, smooth Texas charm and dangerously sexy cowboys?

Crystal Creek reverberates with the exciting rhythm of Texas. Each story features the rugged individuals who live and love in the Lone Star state.

"...Crystal Creek wonderfully evokes the hot days and steamy nights of a small Texas community...impossible to put down until the last page is turned."
—*Romantic Times*

Praise for Bethany Campbell's *Rhinestone Cowboy*

"...this is a poignant, heart-warming story of love and redemption. One that Crystal Creek followers will wish to grab and hold on to."
—*Affaire de Coeur*

"Bethany Campbell is surely one of the brightest stars of this series."
—*Affaire de Coeur*

Don't miss the final book in this exciting series. Look for **LONESTAR STATE OF MIND** by BETHANY CAMPBELL

Available in February wherever Harlequin books are sold.

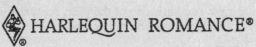

On the most romantic day of the year, capture the thrill of falling in love all over again—with

Harlequin's

Bachelors

They're three sexy and *very single* men who run very special personal ads to find the women of their fantasies by Valentine's Day. These exciting, passion-filled stories are written by bestselling Harlequin authors.

Your Heart's Desire by Elise Title
Mr. Romance by Pamela Bauer
Sleepless in St. Louis by Tiffany White

Be sure not to miss Harlequin's Valentine Bachelors, available in February wherever Harlequin books are sold.

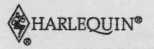

Fifty red-blooded, white-hot, true-blue hunks
from every State in the Union!

Look for MEN MADE IN AMERICA! Written by some
of our most popular authors, these stories feature some
of the strongest, sexiest men, each from a different state
in the union!

Two titles available every month at your favorite
retail outlet.

In January, look for:

WITHIN REACH by Marilyn Pappano (New Mexico)
IN GOOD FAITH by Judith McWilliams (New York)

In February, look for:

THE SECURITY MAN by Dixie Browning
(North Carolina)
A CLASS ACT by Kathleen Eagle
(North Dakota)

You won't be able to resist MEN MADE IN AMERICA!

If you are looking for more titles by

LEIGH MICHAELS

Don't miss these fabulous stories by one of
Harlequin's most renowned authors:

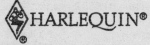